I0691694

THE KILLING HOUR

MARGARET MONTAGUE

BOOK TWO

CHERYL BRADSHAW

This book is a work of fiction. Names, characters, places, businesses, and incidents either are the products of the author's imagination or are used in a fictitious manner. Any similarity to events or locales or persons, living or dead, is entirely coincidental.

First US edition October 2018
Second US edition October 2025
Copyright © 2018, 2025

No part of this publication may be reproduced, stored or transmitted, in any form, or by any means whatsoever (electronic, mechanical, etc.) without the prior written permission and consent of the author.

"I pass my life in preventing the storm from blowing down the tent, and I drive in the pegs as fast as they are pulled up."
   -Abraham Lincoln

PROLOGUE

Margaret Montague moved from room to room, her slippers swishing across the polished oak floors as she made one last inspection. In the sitting room, she paused to straighten a vase of flowers, then stepped back to admire her handiwork. "Yes," she said. "That will do just fine."

Montague Manor, her pride and joy, had stood atop a hill overlooking the lake for more than a century, its white shutters gleaming against the weathered gray stone. At seventy-two, Margaret had cared for the house for almost half her life. Every worn floorboard, every creak of the staircase, felt as familiar to her as her own hands.

After her husband Oliver's passing, there was a short time when she entertained the thought of selling the place. Retirement had its temptations, but the idea of long, idle days didn't sound inviting. What would she do without her guests, without the chatter at breakfast or the endless parade of strangers who, for a few nights, became part of her world?

She paused at the doorway of the front parlor, smoothing a wrinkle from the lace tablecloth as she glanced toward the clock on the mantel. Five minutes to four. Harlan, her latest guest, would be arriving any moment now, and everything had to be perfect.

Montague Manor had seen its share of visitors, from writer's seeking inspiration to couples on weekend getaways, and even the occasional family, but something about her next guest felt different. Though she couldn't explain it, something in his voice during the booking had felt tense and uneasy, unlike her usual cheerful guests.

The chime on the front door sounded, and Margaret turned, smiling as a man walked in, luggage bag in hand. He appeared to be in his late sixties, and she noticed there was a weariness about him. His salt-and-pepper hair was combed, and he carried a faint smell of tobacco, but his eyes—gray, sharp, and distant—carried the look of someone who'd lost their way in life.

"Harlan, I presume?" Margaret asked.

He nodded. "You must be Margaret."

"I am. It's nice to meet you. I trust you found the drive all right?"

"It was long, but yes," he said, his gaze drifting toward the window.

"Well, you're here now. Let's get you settled."

Margaret led Harlan up the curved staircase, her hand brushing over the polished banister she dusted every morning out of habit more than need. The floorboards creaked beneath their steps, the familiar sounds echoing through the upper hall.

At the top of the stairs, she turned left and stopped in front of a mahogany door marked with a brass plate that read *The Ernest Hemingway Room.*

"Here we are," she said, opening it wide with a proud sweep of her arm.

The room was masculine, yet cozy in tone, decorated in deep shades of brown and green. A framed map of Key West hung over the writing desk, along with a few black-and-white photographs of the author himself. The bed, dressed in crisp white linens, was topped with a plaid wool throw. And in the corner sat a well-loved leather armchair beside a tall bookshelf filled with a handful of Hemingway's novels.

Harlan stepped inside, setting his suitcase near the bed as he looked around the room.

"I try to keep each room true to its name," Margaret said.

"It's even lovelier than I imagined."

"You'll find tea and sweet treats in the sitting room downstairs if you're in the mood for a little something later. And breakfast is served at nine sharp. The quiche of the day will be ham and Swiss, which is served with fresh fruit, coffee, and a few other tasty treats."

"Sounds wonderful. You have a beautiful place here."

"Thank you. It's been my labor of love for quite some time now. Now, I'll leave you to get settled in. If you need anything, I'm always around."

She'd just stepped into the hallway when his voice stopped her. "Mrs. Montague?"

"Yes?"

He tipped his head toward the hallway behind her. "That photograph outside of you and the gentleman beside the rose bushes ... was that taken here?"

She nodded. "That's my late husband, Oliver. We ran this place together for over thirty years. He passed three years ago this spring."

"I'm sorry to hear it," Harlan said.

"Oh, it's all right. He's still here in his way, I suppose." She lingered in the doorway a moment longer, studying Harlan as he moved about the room. "Do you mind if I ask, are you married?"

With a quiet exhale, he sat on the edge of the bed, his hands clasped between his knees. "Forty-two years this December. But marriage changes when you stop moving."

"I'm not sure what you mean."

"Now that I'm retired, everything feels different. We have all this time together, and I've realized we don't share much beyond the life we built."

"Maybe all you need is just need a little time to adjust."

"I'm not sure time will be enough. She's a good woman, and she's kind. I love her, and I know she loves me, but the thought of getting a divorce has crossed my mind. It sounds strange to admit it. I haven't said it out loud until now."

"You know, sometimes what feels like an ending is the beginning of something new. Marriage changes shape over time. You may feel unsteady as you step into your retirement years, but I have no doubt you'll find your footing."

"Without my work hat on, I'm not sure I know who I am anymore."

Margaret paused, then said, "Do you read much?"

"I do. It's the reason I chose this place. I like stories that move, fast-paced and full of action. Something with a bit of mystery to solve."

"I might have just the thing. Give me a moment."

Margaret disappeared downstairs, returning a few minutes later with a worn paperback book in her hands. She held it out to him with a smile.

"Here," she said. "This is one of my favorites. *The Killing Hour*. A mystery with a pulse. I think you'll like it."

He took the book. "I'm sure I will."

"I believe books can be good company when our thoughts get too loud. They have a way of quieting the noise, of helping us make sense of things. Sometimes the right story comes along at the right moment and reminds us about who we are, or who we still have the chance to become. Maybe when you've finished this one, you'll see things from a whole new perspective."

THE KILLING HOUR

1

J *uliette*

Juliette Granger glanced in the car's rearview mirror once more, a knee-jerk reaction she couldn't stop repeating, even though no matter how many times she looked, there was nothing to indicate she was being followed. She'd been driving the desert stretch between Las Vegas and St. George, Utah, for the last hour, and given it was the middle of the night, fellow motorists were sparse at best. Even so, she felt nauseous and unsettled— unable to shake the feeling that as soon as her husband Seth realized she was gone, he would do everything in his power to find her.

For now, Juliette took comfort in her biggest ally—time. She'd slipped out of the house an hour and a half earlier as soon as Seth began snoring. Taking every precaution not to rouse him, she'd inched her hand beneath the bed, retrieving a bag she'd hidden earlier in the day while he was out running errands. In that moment, she'd glanced over at Seth before sliding out of bed, horrified when she noticed he had rolled over.

And that wasn't all.

One of his eyes had slid open, and he appeared to be looking at her.

She couldn't move, couldn't breathe, transfixed by the steady rhythm of his chest. Then, with a sudden roll, he turned, and the rasp of his snoring filled the room once more.

Juliette had been planning her exit for the past two weeks.

New place.

New people.

Somewhere safe.

Somewhere no one would think to look.

And most of all, somewhere *he* wouldn't find her.

The buzz of her cell phone on the passenger seat jolted Juliette back to the present, a sharp prickle racing across her skin.

What if it's him?

She hesitated and then flipped the phone to see who was calling, exhaling a sigh of relief as she brought the phone to her ear. "Hey, sis."

"Hey, how's it going?"

"Everything's fine so far."

"Did you make it out all right?"

"Yeah."

"Good. Where are you now?"

Juliette glanced up at a billboard advertising a prime-rib special at a nearby casino. "I'm just getting into Mesquite."

"You shouldn't be too much longer then. I'll let you go so you can concentrate on driving."

Juliette gripped the steering wheel, her mind racing. "Wait, are you still there?"

"Yeah, I'm here."

"I'm worried I made the wrong decision."

"I know how hard this was for you, but if you're unhappy, it was the right call."

"It's just ... I'm scared."

"It's normal to feel this way when you're making such a big change. What did Seth say when you talked to him?"

"I ... umm, I didn't talk to him. I tried to at dinner, but I chickened out. Even now, just thinking about it, my stomach is in knots, and I feel like I can't breathe. I thought about pulling into a gas station and grabbing a soda or something fizzy to settle my nerves, but I think I should keep going."

"Making a pit stop wouldn't take long, maybe five minutes. You should do it."

Juliette wanted to, but the idea seemed like too big of a risk.

She had to keep going.

"I'm ... I'll be fine. Once Seth wakes up, once he realizes I'm gone, he'll come looking for me."

"I hate to say this, but he deserves an explanation, Juliette."

"I know. I left a note. It's not how I intended it to go, but it's better than no explanation at all."

"What did the note say?"

"I told him I was sorry for walking out the way I did. I told him I didn't want to be married anymore, and I asked him not to come after me." Juliette exhaled, her voice heavy. "Maybe I shouldn't have dragged you into the situation. My marriage is my burden, not yours."

"It's not *your* problem. It's *our* problem. You're my baby sister. I just wish you would have told me about your marital problems sooner. I knew you were struggling, but I didn't realize how bad things had gotten."

"I wanted to tell you. I thought about it whenever we talked on the phone. I shouldn't have waited so long. I'm sorry."

If she could do it over, she would have told her sister every-thing from the beginning—everything but the truth about how she'd been living these past four years. But that was out of the question.

Raine had believed Juliette was coming to stay for a while, but she wasn't. She'd come to say goodbye—perhaps for good.

"Don't be sorry," Raine said. "I should be the one apologiz-ing, not you. I've been so caught up in my own life, I haven't been there for you, not in the way I should have. You're a lot stronger than you think. You'll get through this in time. I know you will."

Juliette wasn't so sure.

"I feel like everything's a haze," Juliette said. "My life's a mess. I've made so many mistakes. You have no—"

Idea.

She stopped herself before saying it, knowing the admission might prompt Raine to ask questions she didn't want to answer.

"It's going to be all right," Raine said. "Trust me. How's Nora doing?"

Juliette looked over her shoulder at her three-year-old, snug beneath a blanket in her car seat. "She's asleep. She's got her unicorn, the one you gave her."

"What did you tell her?"

"I said we were going on a trip. She asked where, and I said it was a surprise. She hopped out of bed, grabbed her blanket and her unicorn, and ran to the front door."

"I can't wait to see you both."

"Raine?"

"Yeah?"

"I love you."

"I love you too. See you soon, okay?"

"Yeah, see you soon."

2

Juliette lowered the window a few inches, the phone heavy in her hand. She should have gotten rid of it before she left, but it was a lot harder to do than she'd imagined. Holding it to the night air, she lingered a moment, then let go, watching the last tie to her old life disappear.

Driving on, she headed into the opening of the Virgin River Gorge, a stretch of highway between Mesquite, Nevada and St. George, Utah, known for its steep switchbacks, enormous rock-like mountains, and narrow passageways. She had driven this route hundreds of times, always pressing closer to the window in daylight, searching the river below for the bright shapes of rafters drifting past.

A faint whimper pulled Juliette's attention to the back seat, where Nora was beginning to stir.

Nora rubbed her eyes and said, "Mommy?"

"Yeah, sweetie?"

"I don't want to be in the car anymore. I want Ree-Ree."

"I know you do. Try to go back to sleep. I bet when you wake up again, we'll be at Auntie Raine's house."

"Can she make me strawberry pancakes, the ones with the chocolate sprinkles?"

"Sure, she can."

Nora clapped her hands together. "Yay! I love sprinkles."

The truth was they wouldn't be staying long, but Juliette decided it was better not to mention that just yet.

"Mommy?"

"Yeah?"

"Can you call Daddy? Can he come to Ree-Ree's house too?"

"Not this time, sweetie. We're too far from home for Daddy to come with us now."

"Oh ... kay."

Nora yawned, tucked her head against the car seat, and closed her eyes, leaving Juliette alone with her thoughts again. This time when she checked the rearview mirror, a pair of headlights beamed in the distance, but that wasn't what Juliette noticed most.

The car behind her was going fast.

Too fast.

The speed limit in the gorge was a modest fifty-five.

She guessed the driver was doing seventy at least.

Breathe, Juliette.

Don't freak out.

It's probably some guy in a sports car, treating the highway like his own personal racetrack.

Over the years, Juliette had seen plenty of drivers take this route through the gorge—reckless, foolish people who thought they wouldn't get caught. She'd been one of them once in college, driving through the gorge in her father's pickup with her roommate, Lenore, riding shotgun. As they tested the limits of the pickup, the truck earned its nickname: *The Silver Bullet.*

Glancing in the mirror again, the vehicle was gaining on her.

"Idiot," she whispered. "Hurry up and pass me."

The car approached and then slowed down, switching from the left lane to the right before falling in line behind her.

The driver was at a three-car following distance.

Then a two.

Then a one.

It was as if the person behind the wheel was toying with her, pushing her to speed up, as if he were bored and looking to play a dangerous game.

Please.

Don't be who I think you are.

Please. Please. Please.

Staring up at the sky, it was a starless night, a canvas of black coating the landscape, making it impossible for Juliette to get a clear view of the driver. Even if she could, she doubted she'd be able to make him out through the blinding prism of lights beaming through her back window. His brights were on, and the thick mass in her throat was getting even larger.

She needed to get away from it.

She needed to get away *now*.

Pressing down on the gas pedal, the car thrust forward, sixty then seventy then eighty, way faster than she wanted to go. At eighty-three on the speedometer, she still couldn't shake him. When speeding up didn't work, she adjusted her thinking and did the opposite, easing her foot off the gas. The move seemed to have worked, and the other vehicle swerved back into the passing lane.

You've had your fun.

Now get out of my way.

It looked like the car would pass her this time, and then it didn't. The driver pulled to the side until both vehicles were parallel to each other. Juliette glanced over and squinted. The glow between their headlights gave her a faint view into the other car. When she tried to meet the driver's gaze, he kept his eyes locked on the road. From what little she could make out she could see the driver was a man. He had a ball cap pulled low, sweatshirt hood drawn over it, and sunglasses shielding his face despite the darkness.

Who are you?

Why are you toying with me?

She thought back over the last four years, replaying every choice, every misstep, every consequence that had piled one atop the next. What had begun as harmless fun had spiraled into something dangerous, destroying her life and everyone connected to it. And she had no one to blame but herself.

A single question rose in her mind, one she wished she could dismiss, but couldn't.

Was today the day she'd reap what she'd sown?

3

The back window of the other car crept down, and Juliette's stomach dropped. She bit back a scream, realizing she wasn't facing one man but two. The one in the passenger seat had buried his face beneath a gray beanie, crude eyeholes hacked into the knit, like it had been done in a hurry.

The masked man made eye contact and motioned for her to put her window down.

Juliette shook her head, stepping on the gas as she sped up again.

The driver sped up too, and this time when he caught up to her, the man in the passenger seat had a crowbar in his hand. He shook it in her direction, demanding she pull over.

She clutched the wheel with both hands and accelerated again, and this time when the driver caught up to her, the driver inched his vehicle so close to hers, he almost hit it. In a panic, she canvassed the road, looking for a way out, any opportunity to get away. But there was no place else to go. A heavy metal guardrail was all that separated the highway from the sheer plunge of the gorge below.

With a brutal swing, the masked man slammed the crowbar into Juliette's rear window, shattering the glass and sending fragments everywhere.

Nora's shrieks echoed throughout the car as she said, "Mommy! Mommy! I'm scared!"

"Stop the car!" the masked man yelled.

"No!" Juliette screamed. "Leave us alone!"

He tossed the crowbar to the ground and pushed his body out of the open window, thrusting himself inside the back seat of the car.

"Do yourself a favor, all right?" the man said, his voice steady now. "Pull over."

As Nora's cries broke the silence, the man leaned over, stroking her hair. "Hush now, little one. Don't cry. Everything's going to be just fine."

Juliette jerked her head back. "Don't you dare touch her!"

"I'm only going to say this one more time. Stop. The. Car."

Clinging to the hope he had a rational side, she said, "I can't stop here. There's no place to pull over."

"Don't act like you don't know this stretch of road. There's a pullout just ahead. Take it."

He was right.

There was a small, narrow, dirt pullout around the next bend.

But if she took it, if she did what he asked, what then?

As she tried to come to a decision, she felt something hard press again the back of her head.

"Please, don't hurt me or my child," she begged. "I'll pull over. I'll pull over right now, okay?"

Juliette eased the car to the shoulder and let it idle, her pulse pounding as the other vehicle rolled in behind her.

"Good," the masked man said, tapping the back of her head with the barrel of the gun. "Now turn the ignition off."

Hands trembling, she did as he asked, and he reached a hand toward her. "Keys."

"Why do you need my keys?"

"Just hand them over."

She pulled the keys out of the ignition and placed the keyring in his palm.

"I also need your cell phone," he said.

"I tossed it out of the car several miles back."

"You're not lying to me, are you?"

"No."

The man shoved the car keys inside his pocket and then undid the buckle on Nora's car seat. Wrapping his arms around her, he pulled the child into his arms.

"No!" Nora screamed. "Mommy! Mommy!"

Frantic, Juliette whipped around, reaching for her daughter.

"What are you doing? Stop! Please!" Desperate, and with nothing left to lose, she added, "I know who you are. You may have tried to change your voice, but I still know it's you, Jonas."

He went quiet for a moment, then reached above his head, removing the mask. "Thought this would all be easier if you didn't see my face. Doesn't matter anyway. What's done is done."

"What's done can be undone. Call Max. Call him right now. Tell him I'll come back. I'll do whatever he wants. I won't leave again. I promise."

The man sighed. "I'd take you back if I could, but I can't. You ran. He'll never trust you again. It's too late to change the course of things now."

"It *isn't* too late. I'll talk to him. I'll fix it. He'll understand. He loves me. He's a reasonable man when he wants to be."

"We all have choices in life. You made yours. It's out of my hands now."

"Whatever he's asking, you don't have to do it. You can let

us go, tell him you never found me, and we can forget this ever happened."

"Thing is, it *did* happen, and I'm sorry to say, we both know what happens when he doesn't get his way."

4

Jonas opened the car door slung Nora over his hip, issuing a warning to Juliette. "Stay in your seat and don't move."

Even if he shot her, Juliette wasn't about to let him walk off with her child. She opened the car door and stepped out. Jonas spun around, cracking her on the side of the head with his gun.

Nora's blood-curdling screams rang through the canyon.

"I told you not to move, Juliette," he growled. "Stay put. Don't make this harder on yourself."

Harder?

Nothing could be harder than what was happening in that moment.

Head pounding, she defied his request a second time, reaching out for her child. "Please, give her back to me. She needs me. She needs her mother."

Jonas walked to the other car, opened the door, and placed Nora inside. The driver threw his hands in the air, grunting something Juliette couldn't hear, and Jonas said, "Don't worry about it. I'll handle it my own way."

Nora slapped a hand against the car's window, screaming, "I want my mommy!"

The driver turned around, yelling at her to keep quiet, but she kept on screaming. Jonas turned back, eyeing the driver as he said, "The kid's scared, Victor. Leave her alone."

"Screw you," Victor said.

"Screw *me*?" Jonas said. "Talk to me like that again and see what happens."

Juliette wanted to run to her daughter, to find a way to save them both, but Jonas was heading back over to her now, his gun aimed at her chest.

"Where were you headed?" he asked.

As tears gushed down her face, she said, "I ... I don't know. I just got in the car and started driving."

"Don't lie to me. You've always been a planner, which means you had a plan. I'll bet you've had it for months. I'll ask one more time—*where* were you going?"

"Nowhere without Nora."

"Where, Juliette?"

He had Nora.

What was the point of lying to him now?

"What are you going to do after I tell you, kill me?" she asked. "I thought you were my friend. I thought you were different. You're not. You're just like all the rest of those idiots who work for him."

"This isn't something I want to do. Understand?"

"No, I don't understand. If you don't want to do it, then don't. Let me go, let *us* go. Let us live our lives in peace."

He hesitated for a moment, giving her a glimmer of hope, a glimmer that didn't last long.

"Tell me where you're headed and who else knew about your plans, and your daughter lives," he said.

Up to now, she thought she'd been careful, taking every precaution as she planned her secret escape.

It was all for nothing.

Nora might live, but she wouldn't.

Could she believe him?

Would he spare her daughter?

Her head was pounding, pain shooting in every direction.

"How do I know you'll keep your promise?" she asked. "How do I know you'll let Nora live?"

"You have my word."

"Your *word*? Your word means nothing to me now."

"I have no intention of hurting the child. I mean it."

She backed against the car and looked at her daughter, the tears continuing to flow as she stared at Nora's panic-stricken face.

"Nora's scared," she said. "Please, let me talk to her, just for a minute."

Jonas considered the request.

"Fine," he muttered. "But you're not moving an inch from where you're standing."

Juliette nodded, tipping her head to her side as she looked at her daughter. "It's okay, sweetie. No matter what happens, Mommy loves you, and I'll always love you. Don't cry, okay?"

Nora went silent, rocking back and forth as if trying to self soothe.

"You gonna answer my question now, or what?" Jonas asked.

"I ... yes. I was on my way to Colorado."

"Where in Colorado?"

"Creede."

"Why? What's in Creede?"

"Nothing, it's the reason why I chose it. I didn't think my husband, or Max, or any of you would find me there."

"Max would have found you no matter where you went. Who else knows where you're going and why you left?"

"No one. I kept it to myself."

She blinked at him, hoping the half-truth she'd just told was a believable one. Raine knew Juliette was leaving Seth, but she had no idea about Max, Juliette's secret life, or her plan to move to Creede. Telling anyone would have only put their lives at risk.

"You can't expect me to believe you didn't talk to someone," Jonas said. "Who else knows?"

"I'm telling the truth. I'm not an idiot. I knew if I said anything and my plan failed, I'd be putting the people I care about in danger."

"What about Seth? Why does he think you've gone?"

Juliette thought of Seth, wishing she would have confessed everything to him when she had the chance. "He was sleeping when I left. He knows nothing. Leave him out of it, okay?"

"Do you think I *want* to hurt him, or you? I warned you not to leave. You should have listened."

"I had no choice. I knew he'd never let me go, and I couldn't be around him for one more second. He's a monster."

Victor put the passenger-side window down and leaned over, yelling, "Enough talking! We gotta go. Last thing we need is a car coming around the corner and her making a scene."

Jonas sighed, and Juliette said, "He could have sent anyone after me. Why you?"

His shoulders sagged, and for a moment he stared at her, his expression full of sorrow and regret. "I'm sorry, Juliette. I mean it."

He turned, heading toward the car Nora was in, leaving Juliette confused.

What was happening?

Had he decided to spare her life, to let her go?

There was no life, not without Nora.

"Please, I'm begging you," she said. "Don't take my daughter."

He slid into the passenger seat and closed the door, tossing Juliette's car keys out the window. "Go."

"What do you mean?" she asked.

"I mean leave, head to Colorado. Change your name and never come back. And just know, he'll be keeping tabs on you. If you cause any trouble or speak to anyone about what happened here, you're a dead woman." He pointed toward the road. "You best get going before I change my mind."

She considered her freedom, but freedom meant nothing if they drove off with her child. Racing toward the other vehicle, she yanked on Nora's door. It was locked.

Frustrated and out of options, she pounded on the window. "I can't leave without my daughter! You know I can't!"

Jonas reached out and jerked her toward him, cradling her face in his hand. "You don't have a choice. If you're dead, you'll never see her again anyway. Ten seconds."

"Ten seconds?"

"You've got ten seconds to start your car and get out of here."

"I can't! Not without her!"

The countdown continued.

"Ten, nine, eight."

At the count of three, Juliette did the only thing left to do. She brushed away her tears and ran in the opposite direction, her daughter's screams tearing through her. She swallowed her tears and made a vow: somehow, someday, she would find a way to get her daughter back.

5

R *aine*

Sheets of light shone through the slatted blinds on the window, cascading rectangular patterns across Raine's bare legs. The shapes looked like trapezoids—acute, obtuse—one of the only things she still remembered from high school geometry class.

She'd nodded off on the couch, thinking a few minutes of shut eye would do her some good before Juliette arrived. But she'd overslept. It was daylight, and her sister, who prided herself on punctuality, still hadn't arrived yet.

Raine sat up, taking in the aroma of a decaying floral bouquet she should have thrown out days ago, and then she reached for her cell phone on the coffee table. It was seven in the morning, making Juliette several hours late.

She dialed Juliette's number and waited.

The call went to voicemail.

She hung up, calling two more times and getting the same result.

Her mind began wandering, compartmentalizing plausible excuses so she wouldn't do what she was about to do—panic.

She sent her a text message.

And another.

And another.

Where are you?

Why aren't you here yet?

Why aren't you answering your phone?

Is everything okay?

Call me.

I mean it.

Come on, sis. I'm starting to worry.

Fifteen minutes passed with no word from Juliette. This time, when her thoughts drifted, they didn't cling to easy reassurances. They veered somewhere darker, toward the unthinkable.

As anxiety ripped through every part of her body, she stared at the phone like a mother waiting to hear from a teenage child who'd missed curfew.

The facts were this:

Juliette never went anywhere without her cell phone.

Raine had even teased her about it in the past, always joking about it being the third person in the relationship.

It wasn't like her not to answer or respond.

So why hadn't she?

6

S *eth*

Seth rolled over, sliding his fingers through what he thought would be locks of his wife's hair, surprised when his hand landed on something stiff and crunchy instead. Opening his eyes, he glanced around. Juliette wasn't next to him, but something else was—a piece of paper.

He yawned and pushed himself to a sitting position, reaching over and flipping on the lamp. For a moment, he stared at the folded note, at his name written in blue ink. And although he hadn't read the note's contents yet, he had a bad feeling, one that told him whatever was in the note wasn't good.

Unfolding it, he began to read.

Seth,

After months of struggling in silence, I've come to the hardest decision of my life. I can't be with you anymore. I thought about leaving before, but each time I stayed because you're a good man and a loving father, and because you've given me a life most women would envy.

In so many ways, you are everything I've always wanted. But somewhere along the way, I lost sight of who I am, of what I need, and I realize now that staying has only made that ache grow deeper. This isn't about you failing me. It's about me needing something different, a chance to rediscover myself and figure out where I belong.

You deserve a partner who can love you with the same unwavering devotion you give them. I'm sorry for the hurt this will cause you, for the disappointment, and for not talking to you about this sooner.

I will always be grateful for you, for our life together, and for the love we've shared. No matter where life takes me, just know that a part of me will always love you.

Juliette

Seth read the words a second time, struggling to believe them, struggling to believe she was gone. A rush of memories raced through his mind, and he squeezed his eyes shut, trying to silence them.

Then his thoughts shifted to Nora.

He leapt out of bed, racing down the hall. "Please, please, please let her still be here."

But when he reached Nora's room, she wasn't in it.

He slammed a fist to the wall, shouting, "No! No! No! No! No!"

It couldn't be happening.

Not to him.

"How could you, Juliette? How could you do this to me? To us? To our family? How could you?"

Legs buckling beneath him, he slid down the wall onto the floor, his attention shifting to a framed photo on Nora's nightstand that had been taken months earlier at an amusement park. He reached for it, clutching it in his hands as the memories of that day filtered through his mind. They'd been so happy then. Even when Nora's chocolate-dipped ice cream fell off the cone, staining her dress, she'd clapped her hands when he bought her another, even bigger one.

Where had it all gone wrong, and when?

And how did something that seemed so right go so wrong so fast?

7

R *aine*

Raine's phone buzzed. She snatched it up, hoping it was Juliette, and groaning when she saw it wasn't. She brought the phone to her ear and said, "Hello?"

"Hey, Raine, how's it going?"

Seth's voice was emotional and panicked, indicating he'd found the note.

"Hey, Seth. It's going, I guess."

"Is Juliette there by chance?"

"She isn't."

He went quiet for a moment. "Have you ... uhh ... have you heard from her today, or do you know where she's at? I need to talk to her."

"Sorry, I don't."

She hated lying, but until she knew what was going on, she wasn't sure how much information to give.

"I think Juliette left me," he said.

Raine considered telling him she was aware the relationship was over, but she didn't.

"I'm sorry, Seth. What happened?"

"I don't know. When I woke up this morning, I found a note."

"What did it say?"

"It said Juliette didn't want to be married anymore. I'm at a loss here. I thought everything was fine between us. I mean, our marriage wasn't perfect, but I never thought she'd leave, not without at least talking to me first."

Raine had nothing against Seth. He was kind and reliable, a good husband and a devoted father. But there was no depth to him, no grit or passion. He was safe and predictable. Like vanilla ice cream without any toppings.

"Seth, are you still there?" she asked.

"Yeah, I was just thinking. Sorry. I'm not myself this morning."

"It's understandable. Did Juliette say anything about Nora in her note?"

"She didn't. I don't get it. All their stuff is still here."

"Are you saying Juliette didn't take *anything* with her? Are you sure?"

"She took one thing—our daughter. Can you believe it? She didn't even give me a chance, didn't even let me say goodbye. How could she do that?"

"I ... I don't know."

"All of her clothes are still in the closet, and her suitcases are here. Even if she's serious about ending our relationship, she wouldn't leave without discussing Nora with me. Would she? I feel like I'm in an episode of the *Twilight Zone*."

Raine was aware Juliette had left in a hurry, trying her best not to wake Seth in the process, but not packing her clothes? It seemed odd. If she was leaving him like she said, why not take a bunch of her things with her?

Something wasn't adding up, and now Raine found herself questioning everything her sister had told her.

"Let me see what I can find out," she said. "I'll call you back when I know something, okay?"

"Yeah, fine, but I'm not waiting around. She kidnapped our daughter without my permission."

Kidnapped.

A harsh accusation, but she supposed he was right.

Nora was his daughter too.

Raine was disappointed in her sister for taking the coward's way out. Seth was right. She should have talked to him, handled it better than she had. "I understand why you're angry. Juliette left without offering much of an explanation. I'm sure one of us will hear from her soon."

She'd promised to keep her sister's secrets but given the way everything had gone down with Seth, it didn't feel right.

"I'm calling the cops," he said.

"She hasn't been gone long. I'm not sure there's a whole lot they can do yet."

"I don't care. I need to do something. If you talk to her, can you do me a favor?"

"Sure."

"Tell her I'd like to talk, to see if we can work things out. And if we can't, if she's still determined to end the marriage, then so be it. But she can't just walk off with my daughter. I'm her father. I have rights."

When Juliette first told Raine she was leaving Seth, she never imagined she'd do it without discussing Nora. She thought they'd work out some kind of custody arrangement. When Juliette talked about the note she'd left earlier, she assumed Nora would be discussed.

But she didn't.

Why didn't she?

"I'd also like to ask you for a favor," she said. "Can you hold off on calling the police? Not for long, just for a little bit. Give me some time to see what I can find out. I promise I'll call you whether I hear from her again or not."

There it was—the slip of the tongue.

She'd said the word *again*, alluding to the fact that she and Juliette had already spoken.

It was the exact reason she hated lying.

The question was, had he caught it?

"I give you one hour, then I'm reporting Juliette and Nora missing," he said. "In the meantime, I'm going to head out and start looking for her."

He'd made no mention of Raine's mistake.

She hoped he hadn't noticed.

"All right," she said. "About Nora, I don't believe Juliette would keep you from seeing your daughter."

There was a long pause, and then he said, "Do you know why she left me? If you do, I wish you'd just tell me."

Raine felt for the guy.

He was hurting, and she didn't blame him.

"I think it's best you speak to Juliette about what's happening," she said. "We'll speak soon, okay?"

"Yeah, okay."

Raine ended the call, snatched her keys, and slung her purse over her shoulder. Juliette was out there somewhere, and soon, Raine wouldn't be the only one looking for her.

8

J onas

"I'm not a daycare service. You can't just show up here with a kid, hand her to me, and expect me to take her without explaining who she is or why you brought her here."

Jonas Parr paced the kitchen floor, trying to shut out Sadie's shrill, lecturing voice. Since arriving at her house with Nora ten minutes earlier, she hadn't stopped grilling him. He needed to think, but right now, any brain function he had was being blocked by her incessant yakking.

"Hello?" Sadie said. "Are you listening? Did you hear what I just said? You can't leave this kid here."

He dismissed her with a flick of his hand. "Yeah, yeah. I heard you. Keep your voice down, okay?"

"I'd keep my voice down if you'd start communicating with me and stop making this a one-sided conversation."

"I've heard every word you've said."

Jonas had been on his way to deliver Nora to Max when he had a crisis of conscience, maybe the first real crisis of conscience he'd ever had in his life.

He'd done a lot of regretful things in the past.

Things he wasn't proud of doing.

But today's job ... it was too much.

What did Max want with Nora, anyway?

When he'd been given the order to kill Juliette, find Nora, and bring her back, he'd questioned about the child. Max said it was none of his business. Jonas disagreed.

"Are you going to give me some answers, or what?" Sadie asked. "Something is going on. I want the truth."

He'd learned from experience how fast Sadie's temper could ignite, turning a size-three problem into a ten. No matter how frustrated he was, now wasn't the time to allow her to unravel.

"I want to give you answers, babe," he said. "But right now, I just can't. I need you to trust me and give me a little help with this situation I've been put in."

"I'm the one who's expected to babysit, and I have plans. Whose kid is this, anyway? And why is she with you?"

"I just need you to keep her until I figure some things out."

Sadie jerked her head back, eyes narrowing as she stared into the living room. Nora looked at Sadie, then at Jonas, and she burst into tears.

His heart sank.

Nora used to look at him with fondness.

Now she was wary and afraid.

There'd been a moment outside when Victor left Jonas and Nora on the roadside to chase down Juliette and finish what he'd started. While they waited, Jonas lit a cigarette. When he flicked the last of it into the dirt, he caught Nora staring at him, eyes locked on his, hard and unblinking. He'd never seen that look on her face before. A look of pure, burning hate.

Staring at her now, he was gutted.

"Don't be afraid, sweetie," he said. "I'm your friend. Your Uncle Jonas. Everything is going to be all right."

"*Uncle Jonas*?" Sadie said. "What are you talking about? Are you related?"

Nora ran to Sadie and threw her arms in the air, begging to be picked up. Sadie's expression softened, and she reached down, grabbing her. Nora buried her face in Sadie's shirt, her eyes brimming with tears. "I want my mommy."

Sadie gave the child a hug and set her on the sofa, smoothing her hair back. "Hey, you like cartoons, right? Let's put some on while your Uncle Jonas and I talk for a bit."

Nora nodded, and Sadie switched the television on, flipping channels until she found a cartoon. She turned the volume up and then joined Jonas in the kitchen, hands on hips.

"Does the kid have a name?" she asked.

He nodded. "It's Nora."

"Tell me about her."

"Her mother died this morning."

Sadie slapped a hand over her mouth. "What do you mean? How?"

"It's a long story. I can't get into the details right now."

"Either answer my questions or leave this house and take the kid with you."

Jonas huffed out a frustrated sigh. "Nora's mother got involved in something she shouldn't have, and she paid for it with her life."

"What do you mean? Was she a drug addict or something?"

"No, it's nothing like … it doesn't matter what happened to her. What matters is, the kid's mother is dead."

"Doesn't the kid have a father or any relatives who can take care of her?"

"I don't know."

Sadie's eyes narrowed. "Why do I feel like you're lying to me?"

"I'm not."

"Your right eye is twitching. It always twitches when you're being sneaky."

"I'm not asking you to keep her forever."

"How long?"

"One day, maybe two, just until I figure some things out. I don't know much about her relatives or where they live. She has a father, but he's not an option, either."

"Why did you bring her to me? I don't know anything about taking care of kids."

Jonas threw his hands in the air. "Didn't you ever babysit when you were younger?"

"Umm, no. I'm an only child. I haven't been around kids much."

"Okay, well, Nora is well behaved. You shouldn't have any problems. Make her something to eat, give her a few treats, and then put her to bed in the spare room. It's not that hard."

"If it's not hard, why don't *you* keep her?"

"I can't. It's complicated."

"Why? Because you can't take the kid home to your wife?"

Jonas leaned against the wall, crossing one leg over the other.

He didn't know how other guys did it.

A wife at home.

A mistress on the side.

It was a lot of work.

And not just work.

It was expensive too.

Sadie was the logical choice to take Nora. At Sadie's house Nora would be safe, hidden in a place no one could find her while he decided on his next move.

Take the child to Max, or refuse?

If he refused, there would be consequences.

Was he willing to risk his own life to save the child?

Those questions and others had gnawed at him since dawn.

At the moment, it was more important to convince Sadie to help him.

"I pay for this place, the clothes you wear, the food you eat," he said. "Everything you have comes from me. If I ask you for a favor, *any favor*, I need you to accommodate me. If you can't then maybe it's time we have a serious talk about our relationship."

Her jaw dropped open in shock, then closed with a hard press of her lips as she mulled over his words.

She walked to the table and sat down, patting the chair beside her. "No need to get all worked up. You're wound so tight today. Come sit beside me. I'll rub your back. I shouldn't have lost my temper like I did. You want me to keep Nora? Fine, I'll do it. I'll do whatever you need me to do."

Jonas smiled, relieved he'd gotten through to her. Of course she would keep her. If she wanted to maintain the lifestyle she'd been living, she had no choice.

He took a seat and turned toward her. "No one can know Nora is here. I mean it. No one."

"Why? What's with all the secrecy?"

He raised a brow, and she backed off.

"You can't tell me," she said. "Got it."

"You can't go out, and you can't have anyone at the house until she's gone. And once she is, no one can ever know she was here."

Sadie reached over, massaging the back of his head with her

fingernails. "I get what you're asking. But, baby, I was going to have a few friends over tonight. Why can't I just say she's my friend's kid?"

Jonas shook his head. "Tell your friends you need to reschedule."

"Why can't I—"

"Tell them, Sadie."

She ran a hand down the front of his chest, her long, black hair cascading over his face as she leaned over him. "All right, fine. Is there anything I can do for you while you're here? I haven't seen you in days. You want go upstairs and have a little fun before you leave?"

He glanced at his watch and stood, realizing he'd already stayed a lot longer than he planned. "I'm sorry. I need to go."

Sadie sighed. "Bummer. My bed feels empty without you in it, and it bothers me that you haven't been staying over as much."

"I know, and I wish I could stay. I'll check in tonight or tomorrow when I can."

She went silent for a moment, then said, "Is there any reason for me to worry?"

"About what?"

"I get the impression what's going on with this kid is just the start of a much bigger story. You're not putting me in danger, are you?"

Her naivety, at times, was one of the things that drew him to her when they first met. He brushed his lips across hers, and when he backed away, she grabbed him, pulling him close. "I miss you. I don't like being by myself night after night."

"Once this all blows over, I'll make some time for us. Sound good?"

"I'd like that."

He stood and walked to the living room, bending down

beside Nora. He attempted to kiss her on the forehead, but she recoiled, and he pulled back.

"It's all right, sweetie. I'm sorry about today. I mean it. I'm going to try to find a way to make it right, or as right as I can."

He stood and headed for the door, glancing at Sadie before opening it. "You'll be fine here. Just do what I told you, and there won't be anything to worry about."

9

R *aine*

About fifteen minutes outside of St. George, Raine realized she hadn't seen a single car coming the opposite direction for several miles. It was as if the entire lane had emptied, the highway stretched out like some forgotten road. She craned her neck, searching for other vehicles, but saw nothing.

A few miles down the road, she passed a cluster of highway patrol cars, an ambulance, a tow truck, even a fire truck. All of them were lined up one behind the other on the shoulder on the opposite side of the road.

There was no wreck in sight, but overhead, a helicopter circled, a heavy cable swaying from its belly.

As the scene unfolded ahead, Raine saw two patrol cruisers sealing off the lanes. Three officers stood in the road. Beyond them, a river of cars stretched out of sight, all trapped in place.

Raine's hands felt clammy and slick, and no matter how

hard she wiped them on her jeans, they wouldn't stop perspiring. Her thoughts took her to a place she didn't want to go, a place where she feared the worst. She told herself her sister was fine, that she was just stuck behind the roadblock, but she needed to be sure.

She yanked on the steering wheel, veering off the road and into the dirt. Then she parked and got out, sprinting in the direction of the helicopter. A concrete median split the lanes, and she cleared it in a single leap.

A man leaned against a squad car, his arms folded, wide-eyed, glared at Raine as though she'd lost her mind. The second her feet hit the other side of the road, his hand moved to the holstered gun at his hip.

He pushed off the car and came at her hard. "Excuse me, ma'am. What do you think you're doing?"

Ma'am.

A word meant to show respect but made her feel old.

She wasn't even forty yet.

"It's not 'ma'am,' it's 'Miss.' Miss Raine Hart."

"All right. *Miss* Raine Hart. This isn't a spectator sport."

"I'm not a spectator."

"You can't be over here, and I expect you know that already." He circled his finger in the air. "I need you to turn around and go back to your car."

"What's going on down there?"

"Doesn't matter. It doesn't concern you."

He was tall, muscular, and bald, but unlike most men who lost their hair, the smooth, even shape of his head added to his appeal. He was handsome, and in his early forties, she guessed. His voice carried a rough growl, but his pale green eyes told a different story. They were compassionate and kind, giving her the impression there was a different side to him, one she wasn't seeing at present.

"Has there been an accident?" she asked.

He cocked his head to one side and said nothing, but she was undeterred.

"Why is a helicopter flying so low around here?" she asked.

"Like I said, I need you to return to your vehicle."

"I will *after* you answer my questions."

He stabbed a finger in the direction of her car. "Return to your vehicle, Miss Hart."

Her heavy-handed approach wasn't working, prompting her to try a different approach.

"Please. If you could just let me explain why I'm asking so many—"

He tapped a finger to the holster at his hip. "Not interested. Get moving."

"Could you please stop doing that?"

"Excuse me?"

She pointed at the holster. "You've been thumping your finger against your holster since you charged at me. It's making me nervous. I get it. You have a gun. It's loaded. You don't need to keep tapping it to make your point."

His eyes dropped to his hand, as if realizing for the first time what it was doing. The tapping ceased, though his palm stayed pressed to the holster. "I'm not going to ask you again, and if you don't do what I ask, I'll stick you in the squad car, and you can sit there until I'm done here. Might be one hour, might be several hours. Care to find out?"

She crossed her arms. "It's just, I can't leave until I—"

He grabbed her by the arm and yanked her forward. "All right. Squad car it is then. Let's go."

"Hang on. I didn't *do* anything. You can't just put your hands on me."

"Actually, I can. You refused to do what I asked."

"Who are you, anyway? You're not dressed like a cop."

He released her arm, slid a hand inside his pocket, and dangled his credentials in front of her face. "You know something? You're a pain."

She bit back a smile, but it slipped through anyway.

His name was Will Ford, and he was a detective.

At first, she assumed there'd been an accident. Maybe a wreck on the highway. Or maybe something else—a climber falling from the cliffs, or a hiker in an accident. Something had happened, that much was obvious.

"I'm looking for my sister," she said. "If you would just hear me out, I promise I'll go back to my car."

"I'm busy. I don't have time."

"You're not *busy*. You were just leaning against your car, doing nothing."

Her last comment seemed to anger him far more than her previous ones had, and he reached for her again, escorting all the way to the squad car. She assumed his next move was to place her inside and shut the door.

Then he hesitated, running a hand across his brow. "You have one minute. Not three. Not five. *One*."

A speed round was better than no round at all, and to show her appreciation for his gesture of goodwill, she kept it brief. "My sister and my niece left Las Vegas early this morning. She was on her way to my house in St. George, but she never arrived. I've tried calling her cell phone. She won't answer. The last time I talked to her, she was entering the Virgin River Gorge, but that was hours ago. Something's wrong. I should have heard from her before now."

He glanced at the chopper for a moment but didn't say anything.

"How many seconds do I have left," she asked, "because I can keep going."

He tipped his head toward the sea of cars. "You ever

consider she's stuck in this mess? If you keep driving, I bet you'll spot her. If you don't, you can go to the police station and file a report."

"How long have all of these cars been sitting here?"

"For a while."

"Come on, Ford," she said. "Put me in the ballpark, at least. If you can tell me how long these cars have been here waiting, I'll know whether my sister's trapped in traffic."

He crossed one leg in front of the other and glanced at an expensive looking silver watch on his wrist.

"I can't give you an exact time because we're still trying to figure it out ourselves."

"One hour? Two? More?"

"Several hours. When's the last time you heard from your sister?"

"Around three thirty this morning."

He raised a brow. "What does your sister drive?"

"A Mercedes C450."

"What color?"

"Blue."

"Light blue? Dark blue?"

"I don't know," she said. "Medium blue, I guess."

"New? Old?"

"She bought the car this year."

Her heart raced.

A minute before, he hadn't cared.

Why the sudden interest?

There was a flicker in his eyes, a hesitation, like he was weighing what to say next. Her gaze slid past him to the railing behind the squad car, a ten-foot gap, wide enough for a car to punch through. The metal was bent and torn, as though something had plowed straight across. She jerked free of his grip and bolted toward it, and he lunged after her, catching her wrist.

She spun around and faced him. "There's a car down there. Am I right? That's why all these vehicles have been stopped. That's why the helicopter's here."

His lips parted, and she waited for him to answer, but he didn't.

"Please!" she said. "I'm begging you."

"All right, fine. There was an accident. It doesn't mean your sister was involved."

"Let me look. I need to know if it's her."

"We haven't identified anyone yet. Even if you *think* it's her, right now there's no real way to—"

"Trust me. I'll know."

"If it is your sister's car, it's not the kind of thing you want to see."

"What if it was *your* sister? Your niece? Would you let anyone stop you from looking? Even if you didn't *want* to know, you'd *need* to know, right? What's the harm in letting me look?"

He kicked a bit of loose asphalt with his shoe, thinking. "Tell you what ... I'll let you look if you promise to stick right by me and not take off again. Deal?"

She nodded, and he pointed at a section of railing that was still intact. "We'll look from over there."

He released the grip he had on her arm, and they made their way toward the railing. When they reached it, she shut her eyes, trying to regain her balance. Then she opened them and looked down.

Below, a crowd of people worked in unison, fastening a heavy cable around the mangled wreck of a blue car. The helicopter hovered, its blades slicing through the air as it prepared to lift. The vehicle was crushed, unrecognizable to most, but not to Raine. Her knees buckled as she slapped a hand to her mouth and screamed.

10

S *eth*

Seth Granger sat on the steps of the house he'd built with Juliette, knowing that if their marriage had ended, he wouldn't want to live there anymore. It no longer felt like a home. Not without her. Every wall bore her colors, every fabric her touch. Juliette and Nora were everywhere, and yet nowhere at all.

For hours he'd searched for his wife and daughter, driving in circles because he didn't know which direction she'd gone. Every fifteen minutes he called her phone, clinging to the hope that this time she would pick up.

But she never did.

After returning home, he questioned friends and neighbors, but none of them knew anything. Their shock at her sudden disappearance only deepened his unease. Nothing made sense anymore.

Staring out into the street, Seth watched and waited,

hoping the next car he saw would be hers. Her note echoed in his head. Every word memorized. every phrase dissected. He shouldn't have felt guilty. And yet, he did.

He wondered what he'd missed and what more he could have done.

Perhaps nothing.

It was impossible to know.

Juliette had never been good at communicating her feelings, making it hard to tell when something was wrong.

In recent weeks, he'd detected a sudden shift in her demeanor. She was more clipped with her words and attitude than usual, and when he spoke, he got the feeling she wasn't listening. He'd asked her what was wrong, and she'd shrugged him off, saying it was nothing major, no big deal. But it was a big deal. He could tell.

They'd also had a strange moment three days earlier, when she'd looked over at him as they sat on the couch and said, "You're a good man, Seth. Sometimes I don't think I deserve you."

As he sat lost in thought, a black SUV turned onto the street and disappeared into the garage next door. Seth considered slipping back inside before his neighbor noticed him. The last thing he wanted was another awkward conversation. But before he could, the neighbor was heading in his direction.

"Hey, Seth. How's it going, buddy?"

Seth looked up, admiring how polished his neighbor always looked—fitted suit, combed hair, trimmed beard—the guy always seemed to have it together.

"Hey, Jonas," Seth said. "I've been better, man."

Jonas sat beside him. "You seem upset. What's happened?"

"Juliette left me."

"What do you mean? When?"

"I woke up this morning, and Juliette and Nora were gone.

Juliette left a note, saying she didn't want to be married anymore. I still can't believe it."

Jonas shook his head. "I'm shocked. It doesn't sound like the kind of thing Juliette would do."

"Tell me about it."

"Have you tried calling her?"

"Yep. She won't answer. I've been out looking for Juliette and Nora for most of the morning, and I've spoken to a few of the neighbors on the next street and a couple of her friends. So far, everyone is just as surprised as I am. I thought she might have gone to her sister's house, but we spoke on the phone, and her sister said she hadn't heard from her. I think she might be lying, though."

"Why?"

"Right before our conversation ended, she said something strange. She said she'd call me whether she heard from Juliette again or not. To me, she wouldn't have used the word *again* unless they'd already spoken."

Jonas shrugged. "What's Juliette's sister's name again?"

"Raine."

"She lives in Utah, doesn't she?"

"Yeah, St. George. Why?"

"Juliette mentioned her a couple times. They aren't close, are they?"

"They're up and down. Sometimes they talk almost every day of the week. Other times, weeks go by without any contact." Seth hesitated, then added, "In the past month they've been talking a lot more."

"Seems we're both having a bad day."

Seth turned toward Jonas, brow lifted in question. "What's happening with you?"

"Work stuff. Nothing I can't handle. Anyway, I'm sorry for what you're going through."

"I just don't get it, you know? She may not have been the best at speaking her mind, but to up and leave like she did ... it's crazy to me. And to take my kid without even talking to me first? It's unbelievable. It's like she's having a midlife crisis. She didn't even take anything with her. Her clothes are all still hanging in the closet."

"It's hard to say what made her do what she did. Women are complicated creatures, even the good ones. There's a little bit of crazy in all of them, I think."

Seth ran a hand through his hair. "When I was out of town for work, you and your wife spent time with Juliette. Did she ever mention being unhappy in the marriage?"

Jonas stalled before saying, "I don't know, man. I ... um... well, you know Juliette. It's like you said. She's never been one to talk much about her feelings."

The fact he'd hesitated made Seth uneasy, like there was something Jonas didn't want to say.

"This isn't the time to spare my feelings," Seth said. "You sure she never said a word to you or to Anne? If you know something, I'd rather you just tell me."

Jonas set a hand on Seth's shoulder. "You're a good friend. I don't think it's right for me to speculate."

There it was again, the careful sidestep.

Now Seth felt certain Jonas was holding something back.

"She *did* say something, didn't she?" Seth pressed.

"She may have mentioned a thing or two. Nothing major."

"Tell me. I need to know."

Jonas shook his head as if regretting he'd said anything.

But it was too late now.

"I'm not sure how to say this, so I guess I'll just be frank with you," Jonas said. "Is Juliette taking any medication, or has she ever taken any medication?"

"Of course not. Why would you say that?"

"Last week, when you were out of town for work, we had her over for dinner, and she didn't seem like her usual self. Anne noticed it too. She had a couple glasses of wine, and when I walked her home, she asked me if I ever feel like giving up on things."

"Giving up on *what* things?"

"At first I thought she meant giving up on marriage, but then she said she sometimes felt overwhelmed by life. It made me wonder if she'd ever been suicidal."

Suicidal?

Seth couldn't believe what he was hearing.

"Whoa," Seth said. "Wait a minute. I may not understand the reasons why she left, but Juliette would never take her own life."

Jonas nodded and stood. "I shouldn't have suggested it, and I'm sure you're right. You know her best. I hope I didn't offend you."

Seth swished a hand through the air. "It's fine. Don't worry about it."

"I need to get going, but if Juliette hasn't returned with Nora by tonight, come have dinner with us. Anne would love to see you, and I think it would do you good to have some company right now."

"I appreciate the offer, but I'm not sure I'll have much of an appetite. I haven't eaten anything all day."

"Well, the offer stands if you change your mind. And if there's anything you need, you let me know."

11

J*onas*

Jonas took no comfort in lying to Seth, and even less in the pain it had caused. The pain *he'd* caused. He hadn't meant for things to unravel the way they had, but there was no point stressing about it now.

Living next door to one another over the years had made them more than neighbors, it had made them friends. That bond would be forever changed now, shattered beyond repair, and the blame rested on him.

He'd spent the morning glued to the news, waiting for what he already knew was coming. Juliette's car had been found. It was only a matter of time before Seth learned the awful truth.

Jonas rubbed the back of his neck, the weight of what he'd done pressing down, no matter how hard he tried to shake it off. What choice did he have but to twist the truth, planting a seed of discord when he'd suggested that Juliette was unhappy, suicidal even.

If Seth didn't believe it now, he would soon enough.

Jonas would see to that.

12

S *eth*

Worn out and running on nerves, Seth decided he needed a boost to get through the day. He brewed a cup of coffee and planned his next move. About an hour before, he'd called the police, and much to his surprise, they said they'd send a couple of officers right over.

While he waited, his cell phone rang.

Hoping it was Juliette, he snatched the phone, disappointed when he realized it wasn't her. It was Raine.

He put the phone to his ear. "Hey, I've been wondering when you'd call. Have you heard anything?"

"Seth, I—"

Her voice began breaking apart as if the words she was trying to get out were too hard for her to say.

"What's going on?" Seth asked. "Talk to me."

"I need to tell you something."

Before she could say anything, there was a knock at the door. He opened it and was met by two police officers from the Las Vegas Metropolitan Police Department.

"Hey, Raine," Seth said. "Can I call you back in a few minutes?"

"No, Seth. You need to hear what I have to—"

"I don't mean to cut you off, but there are a couple of police officers at my door. Once I've spoken with them, I'll call you back."

He ended the call, stuffing the cell phone in his pocket. Then he turned his attention to the male and female officers who were standing before him. The male was young and fresh-faced, with clear skin and a trace of awkwardness in his posture. The woman was about twice his age and had bright red hair which she'd pulled back into a sleek ponytail.

She batted her green eyes and said, "Are you Seth Granger?"

"I am."

"I'm Officer MacKenna." She thumbed at the kid. "This is Officer Parker. We heard your wife and child are missing. Can we come in?"

"Yes, of course."

Seth pulled the door open and ushered them into the living room.

Officer MacKenna's eyes moved over the space, as if taking in every detail. Then she turned toward Seth. "When was the last time you saw your wife?"

"Last night. We went to bed, and when I woke up this morning, she was gone."

"Do you remember what time you turned in for the night?"

"It was around ten, I think."

"And what was the last thing you talked about?"

"One of the kitchen lights was still on, and I asked her to

shut it off. She did, and she returned to our bed, and I fell asleep not long after."

Officer MacKenna opened a small notebook and jotted something down, which was too illegible for him to read. A note about him, maybe. Or maybe it was just his paranoia talking.

Beads of sweat dotted his forehead, and he wiped them away with his hand. "I just want to know where my wife and daughter are."

"We understand. The more information we have, the easier it will be for us to do our job. Was anything unusual last night? Did you two have an argument, any unexpected visitors or phone calls?"

He shook his head. "It was a quiet, relaxing night. Nothing out of the ordinary."

"Does your wife have any history of mental health issues, take medication, or have you noticed any recent changes in her behavior?"

He sighed. "You're the second person to mention that today."

"Who was the first?"

"My next-door neighbor. He knew my wife, and he said she mentioned something to him about feeling overwhelmed by life sometimes."

Officer MacKenna made a few more notes. "That's good to know."

"I love my wife."

He wasn't sure why he'd blurted it out.

Maybe it was to convince them he wasn't the reason Juliette had chosen to walk away.

Officer MacKenna cocked her head to one side. "Why do you feel the need to say that?"

"She left me, and I just want to be clear that had I known

what she was planning, I would have done everything in my power to convince her to stay."

"How do you know she left you?"

"She wrote me a note."

He walked over to the kitchen counter, grabbed the note off it, and then handed it over.

Officer MacKenna slid it open, reading what Juliette had written, and then she said, "When did you find it?"

"She left it on her pillow."

"Before today, were there any indications that your wife was planning on leaving?"

He shook his head. "I thought we were fine. I had no idea how she was feeling or what she was planning."

Officer MacKenna exchanged a silent glance with Officer Parker.

"Have you talked to any of her friends or her family, anyone who might have known about her plans and where she's headed?"

"I've spoken to a few people, including her sister. Everyone seems as shocked as I am."

"And your daughter, how old is she?"

"Three."

"What does your wife drive?"

"A blue Mercedes C450."

"Has she ever taken off like this before?"

"No, never."

Officer MacKenna flipped the notebook closed and slid it into her pocket. "Do you have any recent photos of your wife and child that we could borrow?"

Seth gave a small nod and went to the bookshelf. He lifted a framed photograph off it, studied it for a moment, then took it over to the officer. "This was taken just a couple of months ago."

"Perfect. Can I borrow it?"

"Of course."

Officer MacKenna handed the framed photo to Officer Parker and then said, "I think this is all we need for now. If your wife returns, please let us know. Otherwise, we'll be in touch."

They were about to head for the door when Seth received a text message. Reading it over, he said, "Wait."

Officer MacKenna turned back.

"I just received a message on my phone from Raine, my wife's sister," he said. "She's here at the police department, and she's asked me to meet her there. I wonder why."

13

R*aine*

Raine had gone over the conversation she was about to have with Seth a hundred times in her head, but it didn't matter. The truth was the truth, and she couldn't soften it. As she sat inside the police department waiting for him to arrive, a solid lump lodged in her throat wouldn't go away no matter how hard she swallowed.

The moment he walked in, she pulled him into a tight embrace, biting down on her lip so hard the metallic taste of blood hit her tongue. He stiffened like he was unprepared for her affection, and Raine realized they'd only hugged twice before in all the years she'd known him. Once on his wedding day, and a second time when Nora was born. Hugging him now, the embrace felt stiff, like two pieces of cardboard rubbing together.

He stepped back, crossing his arms in front of him. "It's been a long day, and I don't even know what I'm doing here."

"Why don't we take a seat? I'll explain everything."

They moved to a quiet corner out of earshot and sat down.

"Have you heard from Juliette?" he asked.

"I wasn't honest with you before, earlier, when we spoke on the phone."

"Yeah, I kinda figured."

"Juliette called me a few weeks ago, and she told me she wasn't happy. She said she was thinking about leaving the marriage. She planned to talk to you about it last night, but when I talked to her this morning she admitted she couldn't bring herself to do it. That's why she left the note."

He waved a hand in the air. "Hang on. You talked to her this morning, *before* I called you?"

Raine nodded. "About an hour after she left, I called to check on her. She said she had Nora, and they were on their way to my house."

"Why did you say you didn't know anything?"

She flinched at the sharp edge of his words. He wasn't wrong. A thought gnawed at her. Had she, by failing to tell the truth, played some part in all of it?

"What I said or didn't say this morning doesn't matter now," she said.

"Of course it does. It matters to me."

"What you need to know is that Juliette and Nora never made it to my house. After I heard from you, I kept trying to call and text her, but she never answered. I got worried, so after our call, I headed out in my car, hoping I'd catch her somewhere along the way."

"And?"

Raine paused, taking in a deep breath before she said what she had to say next. "When I reached the Virgin River Gorge, I saw cop cars and fire trucks lined up on the opposite side of the highway. A helicopter circled overhead, flying lower than it should have been, which told me something was wrong. I pulled over and spoke to Detective Ford, and I told him I was looking for Juliette. The more we talked, the clearer it became that he knew something."

"Raine, get to the point. Whatever it is, just tell me."

"There was an accident, Seth. A car went off the road. They were using the helicopter to lift it out of the bottom of the gorge."

He gripped her arms, his fingers clamping down until his nails bit into her skin. "Are you trying to tell me … is Juliette … is Nora … are they both …"

She cleared her throat, trying her best to steady her voice. "It *was* Juliette's car that crashed. The weird part is, when they reached her vehicle and looked inside, Nora wasn't in the car."

"What? That doesn't make any sense."

"It doesn't make sense to me, either. Before the crash, Juliette told me Nora was with her, and I have no reason to doubt it. The police have searched the crash site and the surrounding areas. So far, there's been no sign of Nora."

"And Juliette?"

This was the hardest part, the one thing Raine had asked Detective Ford to let her say herself. She thought it would be better coming from her. But sitting beside him now, she wished she wasn't the one delivering the bad news. "I'm sorry, Seth. The drop was too steep. Juliette didn't survive. She's gone."

14

J *onas*

Jonas hadn't always been the most faithful husband, but even he could admit life wasn't worth living without Anne in it. He was sitting at a barstool, sipping on bourbon, watching her hips sway back and forth to the rhythm of a Harry Connick Jr. song while she stirred a homemade pot of marinara sauce on the stove. She looked good in her fitted black dress. So good, he could watch those hips of hers move all day and never tire of it.

One sweet woman.

One spicy vixen.

Between Anne and Sadie, he'd found the perfect combination.

Anne set a wooden spoon in her hand on a plate on the counter next to the stove. She wiped her hands on a towel and turned, raising a brow as if she knew he was eyeing her.

"I see what's happening over there," she said, teasing him. "Stop it."

"Stop, what?"

"Staring at me like you are. You're making me nervous."

He replied with a wink. "After all these years of marriage? You shouldn't be nervous."

"I can't help it. You look like you want to tear my clothes off."

"Well, you're headed out of town after dinner, so we should make the most of our time together, don't you think? I'm not sure how I'll manage without you."

Her cheeks went red. "You'll be just fine. I'll only be gone for two days."

"It's just, your schedule has slowed down a lot, and we've been able to spend more time together. It's been nice."

"It *has* been nice, and I feel the same way. It's just, I promised I'd visit my dad after his surgery, and he's already been home for two weeks."

"I understand. But you know how your dad is when he gets you all to himself. He'll want you to stay longer."

She ignored the comment, grabbed a bowl of salad off the counter, and placed it on the table. "Oh, I meant to ask if you saw the news today?"

"Bits and pieces. Why?"

"A car went off the road in the Virgin River Gorge this morning. They needed a helicopter to lift it out. Traffic was backed up for hours. Can you believe it?"

He raised a brow. "Huh. Wonder what happened. Did they say?"

"They didn't seem to know much earlier, but I'm guessing they'll know more tonight."

"Did they show any footage of the wreck?"

She shook her head. "From what I saw, it seemed to me like

cops were trying to keep the news crews at a distance. I'm sure they want to notify the family first." She dipped a wooden spoon into the pot on the stove, blew on the sauce, and then tasted it. "Mmmhmm. Perfect. I think it's ready."

Jonas had spent the day replaying the morning's events, every wrong move, every slip-up lopping in his mind. The mess was bigger than he'd imagined, a tangle of mistakes that needed to be buried—and fast.

Anne walked over and reached out, running her fingers along his arm. "Hey, you went quiet on me just now. You all right?"

"Yeah, I'm fine."

She smiled. "You sure?"

"I've just had a lot on my mind today."

His cell phone vibrated inside his pocket, and he reached for it, looking to see who was calling. Then he sent the call to voicemail.

"I need to make a quick call, honey," he said.

"Can it wait? We're just about ready to sit down to dinner."

"It's a work issue I didn't get buttoned up today, and it's important. If I don't deal with it now, they'll keep calling. Why don't you dish everything up, and I'll be right back?"

She reached for a plate on the table and shrugged, and Jonas headed toward his office, struggling to maintain his composure.

Anne suspected something was off.

Jonas could tell.

He needed to pull himself together and do a better job of appearing in control. He reached his office and stepped inside, closing the door behind him. Then he made the call.

When it was answered, he said, "I'm sitting down to dinner with my wife, Adam. Make it fast."

"I'm guessing you're aware of how pissed Max is at you right now. He sent you to do a job, and you screwed up big time.

You were supposed to get rid of Juliette, grab the kid, and leave no trace behind. What's happened, it's a complete disaster."

"Yeah, well, the job wasn't easy, and it's not like we had time to plan. We did the best we could given the situation we were put in."

It wasn't the whole truth, of course, but it was close enough.

Jonas had been asked to kill Juliette, but when the moment came, he couldn't go through with it. He'd asked Victor to step in instead, a decision that had turned out to be a huge mistake. Now the police were circling, the evidence mounting, and Jonas had no idea how to clean up Victor's mess.

"Max wants to know about the girl," Adam said. "You have her, right?"

"Why are you the one who's asking? I don't answer to you."

"Trust me, you don't want to talk to Max right now. I've never seen him this angry before."

Jonas sighed. "It wasn't easy, what he asked me to do. It was Juliette, for heaven's sake."

"You're not the only one who had a soft spot for her. We all did."

"It's too bad it had to end this way."

"I agree with you there. I don't know what Victor was thinking, running her off the road like he did. It was reckless."

"If I would have known how he intended on handling things, I never would have asked him to step in."

Jonas had warned Max *not* to hire Victor, but he'd done it anyway, making him wonder if Max hired him to teach Jonas a lesson—to show Jonas all lions had the ability to be tamed if they had the right tamer.

Today made it clear just how flawed Max's judgment had been.

"What should I tell Max about the kid?" Adam asked. "When can he expect her?"

"Tell him I have her, and she's safe."

"And she'll be delivered to him when?"

"Soon."

"*Soon*? Like an hour from now, or soon like tomorrow, or soon like ...?"

When Jonas had driven back into Las Vegas earlier that morning, he hadn't been ready for the storm of guilt that hit him as he headed to Max's house. In the rearview mirror, he saw Nora trembling, clutching her stuffed animal, her face buried against it. He'd made the choice that put her there, and now she was terrified because of it. On impulse, he'd turned the car around, knowing it would only buy him time. Sooner or later, he'd have to take her to Max.

There was no other choice.

Or was there?

"I'll bring her tomorrow, all right?" Jonas said. "Why is Max so interested in the kid? I mean, he's always been fond of her, but I don't get it."

"I don't know. We're not paid to ask questions. We're paid to take care of business. If I were you, I'd get the girl to him tonight, before he gets even more explosive than he is now."

"The kid's been through a lot today, all right? It's one night. Tell Max not to worry. I'll bring her over tomorrow."

"He's not *worried*, Jonas. He's impatient, and you of all people know better than to keep him waiting."

15

R*aine*

Raine and Seth had been at the police station for what seemed like hours. After Raine released her bombshell confession, Seth hadn't uttered a single word, and the silence between them was becoming almost too hard to bear.

Across the desk, Detective Ford and Sheriff Sanders watched them, their expressions heavy with unspoken questions. Raine didn't want to be there beside her sister's husband, a man broken and unwilling to face the truth of losing his wife. What she wanted was to be out searching for Nora, not confined to a suffocating, windowless office.

After a brief period of silence, Detective Ford turned directed his attention to Seth. "We'd like to ask you some questions."

Seth didn't move or acknowledge he'd heard the question,

prompting Raine to tap him on the arm. "Seth, did you hear what Ford said?"

Seth uttered a low sound, something between a grunt and a half-formed word. No one seemed to know what to make of it. Then he glared at Ford and said, "What are you guys doing to find my daughter?"

Ford tapped a finger on the table. "Are you *sure* your wife took your daughter with her when she left this morning?"

"She wasn't in her room or anywhere in the house. Where else would she be?"

"I've spoken to the officers who were just at your home. You didn't see your wife leave with your daughter, correct?"

"I didn't *see* them, no. But that's what happened."

"Is there anywhere else your daughter could be, any friends or family your wife might have left her with, perhaps?"

"I don't think so."

Raine detected a shift in Seth's eyes, his anger mounting, and she cut in. "I don't believe my sister left Nora with anyone. When I spoke to her this morning, she said Nora was with her."

"But you didn't hear Nora, did you?"

"No, I didn't. Still, I see no reason why Juliette would lie to me about it."

Seth shot out of his chair, slamming a fist to the table. "This is ridiculous! There's only one course of action here. Figure out what happened to my wife and find my daughter. All of you should be out there, right now, looking for her."

"Don't assume because the two of us are sitting here talking to you that nothing is being done," Sanders said. "The sooner we get through our questions, the sooner we can get back out there and provide you two with some answers."

"I don't mean to be difficult," Seth said. "I'm just in a place I never thought I'd be, having a conversation I never thought I'd have."

"I understand, believe me. Let's say you're right and your wife took Nora with her when he left this morning. Can you think of any reason why anyone would have wanted to end your wife's life and then take your daughter?"

Seth shook his head. "Is that ... is it even a possibility?"

"It might be. Were there any problems in your relationship?"

"Before today, I didn't think so."

"And you didn't know she was going to leave you."

"I did not."

Ford leaned in close, which Raine suspected was more for effect than anything else. "Then why do you suppose she did?"

"I don't know, and now it seems I never will."

Ford eyed Seth for a time, then changed subjects. "Did you have joint bank accounts or separate ones?"

"Joint."

"Have you ever had separate accounts?"

"Not since we've been together. Why?"

"When was the last time you checked your account balance?"

"Yesterday. Everything was fine."

Ford nodded. "I'd like you to do something for me. Check the account and see if there's any money missing."

"*Money* missing? Why would there be any—"

He stopped mid-sentence, and Raine guessed why. If he hadn't seen her sister's departure coming, then he couldn't predict other things she might have done in preparation.

Seth fished his cell phone out of his pocket. "I'll take a look right now. What do you need to know?"

"All we need is for you to verify your account balance is what it should be."

Seth nodded, entered some information into his cell phone, and waited.

"I look at the account every day. Well, except for today. But today isn't a typical day, is it?" He paused for a moment, waiting for the account to display on his phone screen. "Everything's fine. There haven't been any recent withdrawals, and no new transactions today. Nothing's missing. Why do you ask?"

"You own a black pickup truck, don't you?"

Seth nodded. "Yeah?"

Ford opened a folder, slid a photo of Juliette's smashed-up car in front of Seth, and pointed out the driver's-side door panel. "We found black paint on your wife's car."

Seth stared at the photo, his jaw clenched. "So?"

"We're considering the possibility that Juliette's death may not have been an accident."

"Not an accident? Wait. Are you accusing me of something?"

"We're just asking questions, that's all," Sanders said.

"Sure sounds like you're accusing me of something. Because you found black paint on my wife's car, and I own a black truck, you think I had something to do with what happened to her, is that it? If you're going to start throwing around accusations, this conversation is over."

"Please, calm down."

Seth's eyes brimmed with tears. "*Calm down*? My wife is dead. My daughter is missing, and you're sitting here talking to me about paint. My truck is parked outside. Take a look if you want. You won't find a single scratch on it."

Ford and Sanders exchanged glances.

"If foul play *was* involved, asking pertinent questions helps us rule you out as a suspect," Ford said. "It's protocol, routine questions we'd ask anyone in your situation."

One look at Seth told Raine a panic attack was coming. She'd seen it before—the tightening jaw, the shallow breaths. He'd reached his limit, so she decided to step in.

Looking at Ford, she said, "There's something I should have said when we spoke before."

"Go on."

"I'm a medical examiner."

Ford leaned back in his chair, crossing his arms. "So, you're the one taking over in Utah for Clive Chambers."

"I am. I started last week, right after he retired. Given my position, I have experience in homicides. I understand I have a personal connection to this case. Still, I'd like to be involved."

"It doesn't work that way."

"It *can* work that way, though. If you want us to keep cooperating, to keep answering your questions, it makes sense to me that we work together."

Ford tapped his finger so hard on the desk, she thought he might splinter the wood. "No disrespect, but we're capable of handling the investigation ourselves."

"If that's how you want it, fine. But don't expect me to sit back and do nothing. I don't have a husband or kids,. I don't even have a pet. What I do have is time, and I think you know how I plan to use it."

"Your input is valued, of course, but if you're trying to sway us into giving you what you want, it won't work."

Raine laughed, dismissing his words. "Before I took the position in Utah, I was in Atlanta. I guarantee I've dealt more homicides than you have. I can help you."

Ford crossed his arms, and Raine crossed hers, and for a moment, they sat there, saying nothing. Then Raine pushed back her chair and stood, saying, "Come on, Seth. Let's go."

16

"Now just hold on a minute, Miss Hart," Ford said, jogging toward Raine and Seth in the parking lot. "I have a few more things I'd like to say."

Raine turned. "Why? You made your position clear, and I made mine."

She hadn't meant to come down on him so hard, but the stress of the situation had her worked up a lot more than usual. Her body felt like an internal flame had activated, and it was only getting hotter. Each moment that ticked by without answers was a moment wasted.

And she was done wasting time.

"Give me five minutes," Ford said.

She tapped her foot to the ground, thinking. "It's late. I'm tired, and I need sleep."

"I'll make it worth your while."

"All right, fine. I'm listening."

Turning toward Seth, Ford said, "I'm sure you're worn out from all you've been through today. You don't need to stay."

Seth squished a hand through the air.

"Fine by me. I'm heading home.

He walked off, his head lowered, face forlorn. Raine wished she could ease his pain somehow, offer him even a trace of comfort, but there was nothing she could do for now.

"You should have told me who you were when we first met," Ford said.

"There was a far more pressing issue on my mind at the time, as you're aware. But you're right. I could have mentioned it, and I didn't."

He hooked his thumbs into his belt loops and sighed. "It's too soon to say what happened to Juliette and Nora. I've got a few theories and even more questions. I guess what I'm trying to say is, Sanders thinks it would be good to get your help."

"And you? What do you think?"

"I ... yeah. I wouldn't mind your help, and for it, I'll tell you what I can, within reason. Sound all right to you?"

Raine nodded. "What can I do?"

"I'd like to go back over the last conversation you had with your sister."

She thought back to the call and gave him as much detail as she could remember.

"How did your sister seem to you when you talked to her?" he asked.

"Different than usual."

"Different, how?"

"She sounded tense and scared."

"Any idea why?"

"I told myself the shock of leaving Seth was the root cause. But now, given what's happened, I'm not so sure. I've been replaying that call all day. The words she said, and her tone of voice when she said them. One comment stands out above the rest. Right before we ended the call, she told me she loved me. It was out of character for her."

"How so?"

"She'd always been awkward about saying it. Not just to me, to anyone. I can't even remember the last time I heard her say it, other than to Nora. It's been years."

"People behave in different ways when they experience a heightened amount of stress. If she was in a heightened emotional state, it may have caused her to say things she'd otherwise keep to herself. Would you agree?"

Raine rocked back on her heels. "I don't know, maybe. This may sound strange, but it almost like she was trying to say goodbye, like she had plans she hadn't told me about."

"Huh. Why did your sister want a divorce?"

"She told me she was no longer happy in the marriage."

"Why not?"

"Juliette's always had a hard time letting people in. She was like an onion, every layer peeled away brought me closer to the heart she kept protected. I'm not sure she ever fully allowed anyone into her inner circle."

Ford rubbed the back of his neck. "Not even you?"

"I'd like to believe I knew her better than anyone. Maybe I tell myself that to soften the guilt. I could've been a better sister. I could have talked to her more, done more. I made an effort, but was it enough? I'm not so sure."

"We all do our best, and we all fall short. We're human. It's the trying that counts."

"I thought I had more time, you know? Hard to believe I didn't, that one moment I'm talking to her, and the next, she's ..."

Raine swallowed hard, fighting back the tears, and Ford placed a hand on her shoulder. "What happened to your sister was beyond your control. I've had to remind myself of that on more than one occasion."

He went quiet, his gaze dropping to the ground. For a moment, she wondered if his silence came from recognition, if somewhere in his past, he'd lived through a similar kind of loss. The heaviness in his expression seemed too familiar to be a coincidence.

He cleared his throat, looking at her as he said, "You mentioned your sister kept her feelings close to the vest, but did she ever talk to you about her marriage?"

"She spoke up more in the final months of their relationship, but I get the impression there were plenty of things I didn't know."

"What do you think of Seth?"

"I think he was a safe choice. He gave her a sense of security that made her feel good for a long time. But at some point, I think she got bored of their routine and longed for something more."

"When would you say things began to change?"

"I've been thinking about the phone calls we had over the last few months," she said. "My sister has never been the bubbly, cheerleader type. Her energy was always a lot more mellow. But we had a several calls here and there over the last few years where she was way more upbeat than normal. It was almost like she was trying too hard."

"Trying too hard in what way?"

"Like there was something rehearsed about our conversations. The harder she tried to convince me everything was fine, the less I believed her."

"Did you ever press her to go into more details about her personal life?"

"I didn't. Now, I wish I had."

Ford stared at Raine like he thought it was odd she hadn't checked in on her sister's emotional wellbeing. Maybe it was, but she'd never been one for emotional temperature-taking. She'd always believed if someone wanted to talk, they would.

"I've answered a lot of your questions," she said. "How about answering some of mine?"

The tension between them had eased, and Raine was feeling a lot calmer now. She hoped it was enough to get him talking about the investigation.

"What would you like to know?" he asked.

"You mentioned her car earlier. Aside from the paint transfer, did you notice anything else unusual?"

"Given the extent of the damage, it's difficult to tell what happened before the car went over the edge and what happened after. Did she fall asleep at the wheel? Was there another vehicle involved, a hit and run, maybe? And most important, where is Nora, and why wasn't she in the car when we found it?"

"Is it possible Juliette was forced off the road?"

"Anything's possible at this stage. If another car is involved, we need to figure out whether it was an accident or if we're dealing with a premeditated, intentional attack."

Juliette had never been a social butterfly. She was quiet and private, even withdrawn at times. But she was never cruel, never the kind of person to hurt anyone, not on purpose. She didn't have enemies, and she didn't look for trouble. If someone was involved with her death, Raine couldn't stop asking herself who would want to hurt her and why.

Ford shoved his hands in his pockets. "Hey, while I have you, I want to show you something."

"All right."

He thumbed toward the police department, and they walked in that direction.

"You, ehh, you want a drink or anything?" he asked.

"I'll take a soda. Any kind is fine."

They stepped into the police department, and Ford led

Raine back to the same room they were in before. She took a seat, and he disappeared down the hall. Several minutes passed, and she glanced at the clock, wondering what was keeping him. Then came the faint sound of rubber soles squeaking against linoleum, growing louder as someone approached.

Ford walked into the room with a duffel bag slung over one arm, and a can of orange soda in his hand. He handed Raine the soda, then set the bag on the table. "Does this look familiar to you?"

Raine leaned over the desk, inspecting the bag. "It doesn't. Should it?"

"We found it in the trunk of your sister's car." He unzipped the duffel, pulled the flaps apart, and motioned for her to lean in. "Take a look inside, just don't touch anything."

"I'm well aware of protocol," she said, with a smirk.

She hovered over the bag, her stomach tightening as she saw what was inside, a heap of bundled cash. "Wait, you're saying this money was inside my sister's car?"

He nodded. "Any idea where she got it?"

"No clue. How much is in there?"

"About seventy thousand dollars."

Seventy.

Thousand.

Dollars.

Why would she have that money?

And when in the world had it come from?

"I understand now why you asked Seth to check his bank accounts," she said.

"The money is the most significant thing we found, but there's something more." He opened the duffel's side pocket, reached in, and pulled out a handful of photos. Lining them side by side on the desk, he said, "Do you recognize any of the people in these photographs?"

Raine scanned the photos, each one tugging at a memory she hadn't visited in years. "Yeah, I recognize them. Most of these are from when we were little." Her finger lingered on the photo in the center. "Those were our parents."

"I'm guessing they're no longer alive?"

She shook her head. "My mother passed about ten years ago. After her death, my dad's health began to decline, which didn't come as a surprise. He was lost without her. About a year later, he also passed away."

"I'm sorry."

"Yeah, me too."

"Do you have any other siblings?"

"I don't. It's always just been the two of us."

He shifted his focus from Raine to the other photos on the desk. "What about these other pictures?"

Raine looked them over again, focusing on the one at the end. "This is Juliette and Seth on their wedding day."

"Interesting, don't you think? She took only one bag with her, and it just happened to include a photo of the man she was leaving."

He was right.

It was strange.

Staring at the photos, Raine tried to piece everything together, but nothing made sense.

"Juliette told me things between them were finished, but that didn't mean she stopped caring about him," she said. "I think that's why she left a note instead of talking to him in person. She didn't want to see the look on his face when she told him she was leaving. Hurting Seth would have been the last thing she wanted."

"It makes me wonder if there was another reason she was leaving, one that had nothing to do with him."

"I've wondered the same thing. Is there any way I could see her? I'd like to examine her body for myself."

"You don't think it would be too hard on you?"

"Oh, I know it will. But I feel like it's something I need to do."

"All right, I'll see what I can do."

Her gaze shifted to the bag. "Was there anything else inside?"

"Some makeup, a couple changes of clothes, and one more thing you might find interesting."

He reached in the duffel and pulled out a piece of paper, unfolding it and holding it up in front of her. It was a flyer for a house for rent in a small town in Colorado. A town she'd never heard of before.

"We called the phone number listed on the ad," he said. "The owner said he'd just rented the house to a woman named Jessica Farnsworth."

"Jessica Farnsworth? Never heard of her."

"She was due to arrive last night, but she never showed. According to the landlord, the woman he was renting to was the same age as your sister, and she was moving in with her three-year-old daughter. What I'm trying to say it, I believe your sister was planning to live under another name—Jessica Farnsworth."

17

Raine had spent years standing over the dead, studying faces emptied of life, but nothing could have prepared her for this—for her sister—her own blood, lying cold and colorless on a metal table. She felt her chest cave in, grief flooding her soul.

But now wasn't the time to fall apart.

She had to hold herself together long enough to get through it.

A woman stood across from Raine, her face pale, arms folded against her chest. She was petite, around five feet tall, and her blond hair was braided into a neat bun. She hadn't said much since Raine arrived, except to introduce herself as Sarah Dixon.

"I appreciate you allowing me to see my sister," Raine said. "It looks like you haven't started the internal examination yet."

"So far, I've weighed and measured her, searched her body for any identifying marks, and I've done an X-ray. She has some broken bones and several cracked ribs. I've also taken hair and nail samples. We're running tests now."

"Can I see the body diagram?"

Sarah nodded, lifted the diagram off the desk, and handed it over. Her notes covered the page in cursive loops, but one mark stood out, a question mark drawn beside the right side of Juliette's head. The handwriting was a jumble of slanted lines and difficult to read.

Raine pointed to it and asked, "What does this notation mean?"

"There's a small crack in your sister's skull. It could be related to the crash but considering the placement of her body when she was found, and the fact she was wearing a seatbelt, I'm inclined to believe something else caused it."

"Are you thinking it's unrelated to the car crash?"

"Looks that way. At least, that's how I see it, but I'm not positive yet. You know how these things go." She paused, then continued. "Most of the injuries she sustained were on her left side. The head wound is on her right, and it's toward the back. Nothing the police found at the scene could have caused such an injury."

Raine slipped on a pair of rubber gloves and leaned closer, trying to get a better look at the fracture. It was less than two inches in diameter, and Sarah was right; there were no other wounds around it. Nothing to explain why it was so far apart from her other injuries.

"How long do you think it will take to finish your examination?" Raine asked.

"I'm not sure. My goal is to be thorough. I don't want to miss anything."

"I appreciate it. And I appreciate you for the care you showed her. People don't always think it matters at this stage, but even though her life has ended, it still does."

18

When Raine arrived at Seth's house, he wasn't at home, but he'd texted her earlier, saying he'd gone for a drive, and he'd given her the door code to let herself in.

Whatever had pushed Juliette to leave, the idea that she might have lived under an alias made Raine doubt everything her sister had ever said. Had she really left because of Seth, or was there something else, something darker, that she couldn't bring herself to confess?

And then there was the money found in the duffel bag in her car. The hidden stash suggested Juliette had been mixed up in something none of them knew about. Maybe that was the reason she ran.

Raine entered the house, walked down the hall to Nora's room, and flipped on the light. She opened her closet and rows of dresses greeted her—soft colors, delicate fabrics, each one holding a different memory. She reached for one she recognized, the same dress Juliette had sent her a photo of a month earlier. The fabric was cool beneath her fingers. She brought it to her face and inhaled, catching the faint trace of vanilla and lavender.

The tears came, and she didn't fight them. She wished she could turn and see Nora beside her instead of standing there, hollow and lost, wondering where her niece was, and if she'd ever see her again. She closed her eyes and pictured Nora alive, because believing otherwise was something she couldn't bear —not unless she had no other choice.

Raine hung the dress back up and went to the master bedroom, finding it neat and tidy. The clothes in Juliette's closet had been hung according to color, light to dark from left to right. She searched inside, looking for anything that seemed out of the ordinary, but everything appeared to be as it should have been.

Seth was right.

Juliette *had* left everything.

There were no empty hangers, no empty drawers, no spaces that looked like anything had been removed.

It was like she'd left with every intention of returning.

At face value, nothing inside the house stood out as a red flag, except for the unsettling fact that there *weren't* any red flags.

If Raine wanted answers, she needed to dig deeper.

She grabbed a chair from the kitchen table, returned to the closet, and stood on it, reaching for the shoeboxes lined on a shelf above her clothes. The boxes contained a lifetime of memories—photos, awards, journals—all spanning the last thirty years. They were precious mementos Juliette had saved, items like the photos she'd stashed inside the duffel bag that she assumed she wouldn't have left behind.

So why had she?

Beside the shoeboxes were three pink luggage cases. She pulled them down, one by one, assuming they would be empty, and two of them were. But the weight of the largest one suggested otherwise.

She pulled the suitcase off the shelf, tipped it on its side, and pulled on the zipper. The lid flopped open, spilling a handful of dresses onto the floor. She picked one up and held it out in front of her. It was short, black, and strapless, and *not* the way her conservative sister had ever dressed.

Raine sifted through a few more dresses, each one similar in style to the black one, until she came to a red dress. It had pockets, something Juliette always loved, and one of the pockets wasn't lying flat. Curious, she slipped her hand inside, gasping as she drew out a diamond and sapphire tennis bracelet.

The stones on the bracelet looked real.

Seth's income was modest, enough to cover the bills and keep them comfortable. And jewelry had never been his thing. Aside from her wedding ring, Raine didn't recall him ever giving her any other jewelry.

If Seth hadn't given her the bracelet, who had?

And why?

As she pondered those questions, there was a knock at the front door.

She wondered if it might be the police, but it was late, too late for a typical house call in Raine's opinion.

Raine slid the bracelet into her pocket, stuffed the dresses back into the suitcase, and returned it to the shelf.

Halfway to the door, she stopped, deciding to err on the side of caution. She didn't know who was on the other side of that door. And given the suspicion around Juliette's death, she decided to retrieve the handgun she always carried in her handbag.

Raine tucked the gun into the waistband of her jeans as another knock sounded. It was much louder this time.

She approached the door and flipped the porch light on, but she didn't open it. "Hello? Who's there?"

"Uhh ... hi. It's Jonas."

It's Jonas was *not* the police.

"Who are you?"

"Seth's neighbor."

Jonas.

Raine recalled Juliette speaking about him and his wife, but they'd never met.

"What can I do for you?" she asked.

"I was wondering if Seth was around."

Juliette may have spoken about Jonas in a favorable way, but Raine didn't know him, and she hesitated to admit she was there alone.

"Seth will be here any minute," she said.

It went quiet for a moment, and Raine wondered if he'd gone.

Then he said, "I saw you arrive. Who are you, if you don't mind me asking?"

"Why does it matter?"

"No reason. I was just curious. I saw Seth earlier today. He told me about Juliette. He said something about not having much of an appetite, but my wife made some pasta, and she wanted me to bring it over."

Raine crept over to the window and peeked outside, catching sight of the dish in his hand.

Headlights approached, illuminating the living-room wall as a truck came to a stop in the driveway. Seth was home, and Raine was relieved to see him.

Jonas stepped off the front porch and walked over to Seth as he got out of his truck, handing him the casserole dish. They did a one-armed embrace and began chatting. Unable to hear what they were saying, Raine decided to join them.

As she approached, Seth glanced at her, then back at Jonas. "Have the two of you met?"

"We were just getting to that before you arrived," Raine said.

"Jonas, this is Raine, Juliette's sister," Seth said.

"Ahh," Jonas said. "I've heard a lot about you."

Jonas shot Raine a wink, a gesture suggesting there was familiarity between them even though there wasn't. He struck Raine as the kind of guy who thought charm could get him anywhere. But that wouldn't work, not on her.

"Have you heard from Juliette yet?" Jonas asked.

Seth went quiet, his gaze fixed on the dish in his trembling hands.

Jonas seemed to pick up on the fact his question hit a nerve, and he said, "Oh, man. I guessing it isn't good. I'm so sorry."

Jonas seemed unaware of Juliette's tragic end, but was he?

Given the recent details that had come to light, Raine found herself unwilling to trust anyone, not until they proved they could be trusted.

She thought about how best to explain what happened to her sister, and in the end, she decided on a simple, blunt approach to see how he'd take it.

"Juliette was in a car accident this morning in the Virgin River Gorge," Raine said.

"What do you mean?" Jonas asked.

"We don't have all of the details yet."

"Where is she now, in the hospital?"

"I'm sorry to say she didn't survive."

"I can't believe it," Jonas said. "We were just catching up yesterday. And Nora?"

"She's missing."

"What do you mean? If the car was found and you know what happened to Juliette, how is it Nora—"

Raine cut in, offering Jonas a brief overview of the day's events.

When she finished, he shook his head in disbelief. "I can't believe this is happening. Do the police know what caused the accident?"

"They're following up on a few leads."

"You've spoken to them then?"

"We both have. Right now, they're trying to figure out whether the incident was an accident or whether Juliette was forced off the road. We expect to hear something soon."

Seth set the casserole dish on the hood of the truck and leaned against it. "I've been doing a lot of thinking this evening, and there might be a third option."

"What are you talking about?" Raine asked.

"I hate to even mention it without knowing if there's any truth to it, but earlier today Jonas told me Juliette had been depressed, or he thought she was, at least," Seth said. "He suggested she may have taken her own life."

Raine's nostrils flared, rage growing inside her.

She glared at Jonas, wanting nothing more than to slap him across the face for making such a suggestion.

"Uhh, no," she said. "No way that's true."

Jonas raised his hands. "Hey, it was just an observation. I didn't state a fact. No need to get upset."

"Because you two were neighbors, you think you know everything about her now? What gives you the right—"

Seth cut in. "Hang on, Raine. Juliette said a few things to Jonas in confidence. Things I didn't know about until today."

"What *things*?" Raine asked.

Jonas shrugged. "She made a comment about wanting to give up. It sounded to me like she wasn't happy in her life."

Raine placed her hands on her hips, forcing herself to keep the anger simmering inside from boiling over. "I don't know you, Jonas, but what I do know is that Juliette isn't here to defend herself or to say whether she even made such a comment. Perhaps you should keep your assumptions to yourself."

"She told *me*, not you," Jonas said. "I stand by what I told Seth."

"And I stand by saying it isn't true. Either way, I'm done talking."

Raine pivoted and started toward the house.

Jonas rushed after her, reaching out and grabbing her arm. "Hang on a minute. I didn't mean to offend you. I'm sorry. I shouldn't have been so inconsiderate after what you've been through today."

Raine shrugged him off. "You gave your opinion. I just don't agree with it."

"Until we have answers, maybe we shouldn't speculate," Seth said. "Besides, the police think it's possible there was another vehicle involved."

Jonas whipped around, a look of shock on his face. "What are you saying? What makes them think that?"

"They found black paint on the driver's-side door of her car. They're running tests on it."

"What kind of tests?"

Seth thumbed in Raine's direction. "Ask the medical examiner. She knows way more about this stuff than I ever will."

"Metal bends on impact," Raine said. "If a vehicle is at an angle when it's hit or if there's friction between one car and another, there's inevitably going to be paint transfer."

Jonas shook his head, confused. "Paint transfer?"

Raine paused, trying to think of a simpler explanation, one he could understand. "Have you ever parked next to a metal pole and noticed it was marred with several different colors? It happens when vehicles scrape up against it, thus creating a transfer of paint from one object to another."

"Even if there's paint on Juliette's car, how does it prove another car was involved?" Jonas asked.

"Most auto manufacturers apply four coats of paint and primer to their vehicles. When a lab runs forensic tests on a paint chip, they look for the order in which the paint was applied and how many layers were applied. Sometimes it helps them locate the other vehicle involved."

A flicker of concern, or maybe surprise, crossed his face, a shift from his earlier demeanor. Raine couldn't place it, but it unsettled her. She didn't like him, and she was anxious to end the conversation.

"I'm tired," she said. "I'm going to call it a night."

"Me too," Seth said. "And hey, thanks for the pasta."

As Seth started for the house, Jonas gave his shoulder a quick pat. "I just want to say again how sorry I am. If you need anything, you know where to find me."

19

J *onas*

Paint chips. Paint transfer. Multiple coats of paint.

Jonas felt like he was on a merry-go-round that was spinning out of control. In the past, his kills were always clean—planned, simple, precise. A bullet to the head, followed by a meticulous disposal of the body, and just like that, the person ceased to exist.

No body.

No evidence.

No trace.

Juliette's murder was impulsive and chaotic. There hadn't been time to plan, and because of that, now he was paying the price. Worse, he hadn't counted on how sloppy Victor would be when he killed her. There would be blowback from Max. He just didn't know how bad it would be.

As the weight of it all came closing in on him, his thoughts spiraled. He swung hard, his fist connecting with the stucco wall on his front porch. Pain shot up his arm, and he cursed under his breath for trusting Victor to do a job he should have done himself.

His rage burned hot, then dissolved as Juliette's face surfaced in his mind. Against his will, a trace of sentiment crept in.

How could it not?

She wasn't just another job, another name to erase.

She was a friend.

His friend.

The thought of what he'd been tasked to do made him sick.

And then there was the sister.

Who knew she was a medical examiner?

If Juliette had mentioned it before, he hadn't remembered it.

As his stomach churned, tense and uneasy, his cell phone buzzed. He took the call, grunting a sound of disgust as he saw the name on the Caller ID.

"What now, Adam?" he grumbled.

"Turn around."

Jonas looked over his shoulder and saw nothing. The street was quiet. He was alone. At least, he appeared to be. "Why? What do you want?"

"Do you see me?"

"It's ten o'clock at night. How could I?"

The high beams of a car flashed on and off. "I'm parked at the end of the street. Do you see me *now*?"

Jonas sighed. "Why are you here?"

"We need to talk."

"No, we don't. Not tonight. You know better than to show up at my house."

"Yeah, well, I'm not leaving until I talk to you. Orders are orders."

"We agreed never to meet at each other's homes. What if my wife had been here?"

"Yeah, but she's not, is she? She's visiting her father, isn't she?"

"How do you know that?"

"Could have sworn you said something to me about it."

Jonas was certain he hadn't.

How long had Adam been sitting on the street, watching and waiting?

The mess he'd made seemed to keep getting messier, and now Adam had crossed a line.

Time to put a stop to it.

Jonas sprinted toward Adam's car, adrenaline pulsing through his veins. He yanked the passenger door open and slid inside, pressing a gun to Adam's forehead.

Adam attempted to smack it away, saying, "Calm down. I'm just following orders, same as you. If you're angry, it's not on me."

"We had an arrangement. I do the jobs I'm assigned, and I'm left alone. My private life is private. I don't come to your house, and you don't come to mine. Ever."

"I'm aware, Jonas. We all have the same arrangement."

"Then you shouldn't be here."

"Do you think I *want* to be here? Max sent me. You shouldn't be surprised. Get this gun out of my face, and we can talk."

Jonas eased back, the gun still in his grip, no longer aimed at Adam but ready if he needed it. "Go ahead then, talk."

"Max spoke to Victor, and do you want to know what he said? He told Max that *he* took care of Juliette, *not you*. It's no wonder the situation has turned into complete chaos. You didn't follow the plan. And Max ... well, if you thought he was mad before, imagine how he's feeling now."

Victor—the little snitch.

He'd snap his neck when he saw him.

Jonas had despised Victor from the moment they met. It should've been Victor at the bottom of the gorge, not Juliette. It was only a matter of time before Max discovered even more disturbing truths. Jonas just hoped he'd have time to cover his tracks before that happened.

"So what if Victor finished the job," Jonas shrugged. "It got done. That's what matters."

"The police are poking around, and her death is national news. Do you see the problem here? There's a car, a body, *and* an investigation led by some prick named Ford who has a reputation for never knowing when to quit. He's not going to let this go."

"How many homicides could this guy have under his belt? He's a detective out of Mojave County, right?"

"He is now. Used to work in Suffolk County."

Suffolk County was in New York.

Not good.

Adam's new tidbit of information was troublesome. Still, Jonas had to believe there was a way to save face. "I didn't know Victor was going to go off-script. I told him what to do, and he didn't do it. When I learned about what happened, it was too late."

"That's funny."

Jonas jerked back. "What's funny?"

"Victor said you had the perfect opportunity to take care of Juliette yourself, and you wasted it, asking him to take care of her instead."

"He offered, and I thought he could handle it. I was wrong."

Adam tossed his arms in the air. "He's not a professional

like we are. Not yet. You should have never let him go after her alone."

"I'll find a way to get us out of this mess. I always do."

"Yeah, well, whatever you plan on doing, you better do it fast. Where's the car you tailed her in?"

"I scrapped it. Max doesn't need to worry. It will never be found."

Adam glanced out the window then back at Jonas. "Max sent me here to get the kid."

"You think I'd bring her here, when her father lives next door? She's somewhere safe. I'll bring her over tomorrow morning. If he's got a problem with that, he can call me himself."

Jonas pushed the door open and stepped out, the night air cool against his face. He lingered for a moment, one hand on the roof of the car, letting the silence stretch long enough to make Adam squirm. He wanted him to feel it, the shift in power, a reminder of who was in charge here.

He turned back, his voice low and cold. "Don't ever show up at my house uninvited again. Next time, I won't be so lenient."

20

R *aine*

Raine removed the large suitcase from Juliette's closet and showed Seth the dresses she'd found inside. He picked through them, examining each one with more disapproval than the last.

"These aren't Juliette's clothes," he said. "They can't be. You know they're not. She'd never dress this way."

"But they're here, in *her* suitcase."

He shook his head. "Well, I can't make sense of it."

"I guess I'm just a little surprised that you didn't know anything about this other life of hers."

He leaned over the pile of dresses and sighed. "Do you blame me? Do you think if I would have paid more attention to her, if I would have been more involved in her life, or if I didn't work out of town, I could have kept this from happening?"

In recent years, Raine hadn't considered herself a gold-star sister. Maybe a silver on a good day when Juliette called, but

Raine didn't reach out as much as she should have. She told herself her sister didn't need her the way she used to, when they were younger. Thinking about it now, maybe Juliette went quiet because she'd changed, her life had changed, a life she was trying to keep hidden.

Seth bent down, lifting the red slip dress from the pile. "Look at this thing. There's nothing to it. It's lingerie disguised as a dress."

If he thought that was bad, it was about to get worse.

Raine pulled the bracelet she'd found out of her pocket and showed it to him. "Have you ever seen Juliette wear this before?"

He squinted, leaning in for a closer look. "I have, yes."

"How long ago?"

"You should know."

"How would *I* know?"

Seth studied Raine's face for a time and then picked the bracelet out of her hand, dangling it in front of her. "Juliette told me it was a gift from you for her birthday."

"I'm sorry, Seth. I didn't buy it for her."

His focus shifted back to the bracelet. "What about these gems? Do you think they're real?"

"I believe they are, and it looks like it's worth a lot of money."

"How *much* money do you think?"

"In the thousands, I'd guess."

"Are you sure?"

"I've bought enough jewelry to know that this bracelet looks expensive."

Seth wadded the bracelet inside his hand and threw it across the room. Then he walked to the bed and sat down, covering his face with his hands. "I feel like I'm losing it. I don't know what's real and what isn't anymore. It's like I've stepped into someone else's chaotic life. How is this *my* life? How can it be?"

Raine hopped up, sitting beside him. "You're not alone. I feel the same way. It wasn't like Juliette to be dishonest about anything, but from what it seems, she lied to both of us."

"One lie after the other. I wonder how many things we still don't know."

"Here's one thing. After you left the police department, and I was speaking with Ford, he showed me something, a duffel bag they found in Juliette's car. It was filled with cash and a bunch of sentimental photos."

"What was she doing driving around with a bunch of cash?"

"I don't know. I wish I did."

As the day had gone on, Raine allowed her mind to wander, taking what she knew about the case and creating scenarios. Seth was gone for work several days each week, and it occurred to Raine that her sister might have been living a double life, one hidden from everyone who knew her.

"I have a question," she said. "When you were out of town for work, what was Juliette's routine?"

He gave the question some thought. "She played tennis at Bellevue, hung out with friends, and visited your aunt at the assisted living facility in Henderson."

Aunt Cora, their mother's sister, had been diagnosed with Alzheimer's disease four years earlier. She'd never had any children of her own. At the onset of the disease, Cora had gifted Juliette a large sum of money, which Juliette had used to buy their house.

Raine was gifted a much smaller amount. She told herself it was because she didn't need the money like Juliette did, but in truth, Juliette had always been Cora's favorite.

Why?

Growing up, Juliette was well behaved and obedient.

Raine was mouthy, though she found it interesting how time had changed them both.

"It's been a long time since I've visited Cora," Raine said. "How is she doing?"

"About the same. Juliette believed Cora had lucid moments where she remembered her, but the few times I visited your aunt, she acted the same way she always did—checked out of life. I don't think she recognizes anyone anymore." He paused, then said, "Hey, can I ask you something?"

"Sure."

"I get the feeling you know a lot more about Juliette's decision to leave me than you let on earlier. Did she tell you why she made that decision?"

"She said she was unhappy, and all this time I assumed she was talking about your marriage. But now, I'm not so sure. I tried to get her to talk more about it, and she said she'd go into more detail when we were face to face."

He shook his head. "Typical Juliette."

"Juliette didn't have many friends, did she?"

"She had a few, but she didn't like going out. That's what makes the dresses you found so unusual. They look to me like, you know, something a woman would wear in a nightclub."

"When you were away for work, what did she say she was doing?" Raine asked.

"Most of the time she said she was at home, or out doing things with Nora. Jonas and his wife would check in on her, invite her over for dinner, and things like that. But I found what he said today strange. Why would Juliette shut us out and turn to our neighbor instead?"

"I'm not sure. All I know is, Juliette didn't take her own life."

"I know your first impression of Jonas wasn't favorable, but he isn't a bad guy."

Time would tell.

The idea that Juliette would consider taking her own life was absurd. Nora was her whole world. No matter how low dark things may have gotten, she never would have allowed her child to grow up without a mother.

Raine hopped off the bed and walked over to the suitcase, shoving the dresses back inside. She zipped it closed and turned. "Jonas asked a lot of questions either. I know you consider him a friend, but how much do you know about him?"

Seth leaned back on the headboard, lacing his hands together behind his head. "Well, let's see. He moved in right after we did, and he's spent a lot of time around us. He's always been a stand-up guy, a good friend to our family, and his wife is one of the kindest people I've ever known. They're a great couple."

Maybe Jonas *was* a decent guy. Then again, Seth was the kind of person who always saw the best in people. He was quick to trust and easy to forgive—two traits Raine lacked.

"I'm not sure how long it will take us to get the answers to our questions," Raine said. "But I won't stop searching until I find out what happened to Juliette and to Nora."

Seth nodded. "I guess we should talk about what happens now. What are your plans? Are you going back to St. George, staying in Las Vegas, or ...?"

"I'd like to stick around for a while. I'll get a hotel, and we can check in with each other each day and compare notes."

He swished a hand through the air. "You don't need to go to a hotel, Raine. We're family. Why don't you stay here for now? You can sleep in Nora's room."

Raine appreciated the offer, but Seth was grieving, and she was unsure if her presence would bring him comfort or make things worse.

"I don't know," she said. "Are you sure?"

"I am. We could work together. Besides, it may sound selfish, but I'd rather you were here. Without you ... well, I'm afraid it will be too quiet, and the last thing I need is to be alone with my thoughts right now."

It didn't sound selfish at all.

It sounded like he was taking a big step in self-care.

Raine headed toward the bedroom door. "I appreciate your offer, and I accept. It may sound weird but being in this house around Juliette and Nora's things is helping me stay sane. We may not have the answers now, but they're out there, waiting to be found, and something tell me when we do, our lives will change forever."

21

J *onas*

All was quiet, but would it stay that way? Adam's unexpected visit had left Jonas on edge, wondering if he was still out there somewhere, watching every move he made.

Jonas had always had a good relationship with Max, but today that relationship had been fractured. He could feel it. The shift was palpable, and for the first time since he'd started working for Max, he felt a growing feeling of distress.

In the past, they'd always had a mutual respect for each other. He liked to think they did, at least. Then again, Jonas had never let Max down before. He'd always done what Max asked, when Max asked. No questions asked.

The consequences were coming.

He could feel that too.

And it wasn't hard to grasp the price he'd pay for defying an order.

As he pondered those thoughts, he noticed the lights in Seth's house were still on, and Raine's car was still parked in the driveway, indicating she was spending the night. It was yet another reality that made him restless.

Raine was trouble.

Jonas sensed it the moment they met.

While petite, she was packed with determination. There was fire in those big, blue eyes of hers, and when she looked at him, it was like she could see right through him, like she *knew* he was hiding something.

She needed to leave, sooner than later, but Jonas was tired, and he decided he'd revisit the idea of what to do about her tomorrow.

His cell phone rang, and every fiber in his being wanted to let the call go to voicemail. He had a good idea of who would be on the other end of the line, and he hadn't come up with the right words to say yet.

He reached for his phone on the counter and answered.

"Why didn't you bring Nora today like I asked?" Max asked.

"Have you spoken to Adam?"

"What do *you* think?"

"The kid is a mess, and given it's the middle of the night, she's all tuckered out. I'll bring her by tomorrow."

"She can be tuckered out at my house. What's the reason for the delay?"

He paused, knowing he needed to come up with a better answer.

Remain calm.

Keep your voice steady.

You got this.

"Nora was terrified when we picked her up," Jonas said. "She wouldn't stop screaming. I thought since she knows me, if I spent a little extra time with her, I could help her to calm down. I gave her some ice cream, bought her a few toys, and while I wouldn't say she's okay, she's better than she was before."

All lies.

The question was, did Max believe him?

"Did anyone see you with the girl?" Max asked.

"No one."

"How can you be sure?"

"I put a wig and a hat on her."

More lies.

"You *will* bring her to me first thing in the morning," Max said. "Do you understand?"

"I do."

"Good. I have another job for you."

Jonas brushed past the job request and asked the one question that had been gnawing at him all day. "Why do you want the kid? What are you planning to do with her?"

"It's none of your concern. She'll be safe here with me. You don't need to concern yourself about it."

Jonas knew better.

No one was *ever* safe in Max's orbit no matter what kind of assurances he offered.

Juliette's murder was a perfect example.

And yet, in the years he'd worked for Max, he'd never known him to harm a child. Even Max had his limits, it seemed.

"What's the job?" Jonas asked.

"Because of your screw up, the police are looking for Nora, and they're investigating Juliette's murder. I have a feeling that pesky husband of hers is going to turn his house upside down looking for answers once it all settles in.

You need to get rid of him before that happens."

"No offense, but it isn't smart, Max. Killing him will only bring more suspicion to the case."

"For now, perhaps. The way I see it, it's best to tie up loose ends while we have the chance. I have no doubt the police are going pursue every lead, and once they do, they'll exhaust their resources. Attention to the case will fade, and without any solid leads, it will all die down. You'll see."

Jonas had always found Max to be one of the most level-headed men he knew, until now. It was like something inside him had snapped, and all sense of reason was gone.

"Seth is innocent in all of this, I swear," Jonas said. "He doesn't deserve to die for Juliette's mistakes."

"Since when do you care whether someone deserves it or not? Who knows what Juliette left behind? You need to take care of him and the sister-in-law if she's still there. Then do a complete sweep of the house, removing anything that could tie the police back to me."

Jonas lowered the phone, desperate to find a way out of what Max had demanded, but once Max made a decision, there was no escaping it.

"This isn't who we are," Jonas said. "This isn't what we do."

"Who we are and what we do changed when you let Victor finish the job for you. You have yourself to blame for what happens next."

Defeated and out of ideas, Jonas said the only thing he could think to say. "All right, I'll do it."

"It's settled then. I'll see you in the morning. We have much to discuss."

The line went dead, and Jonas inhaled what felt like the first breath he'd taken in several minutes.

First Juliette.

Now Seth and Raine.

It was all getting to be a bit too much.

The women.

The jobs.

The money.

There was a time he'd taken pride in the work, never hesitating when a job came his way. He didn't know when that shifted, only that it had. Maybe he was losing his edge. Or maybe he'd realized it wasn't worth it anymore. He had it all—money, comfort, a loving wife.

Perhaps Juliette had the right idea all along.

Perhaps it was time to cut ties and run himself.

22

S adie

The hallway went on forever, lined with doors, every bell blaring at once in a piercing, discordant chorus. The noise drilled through Sadie's mind until her eyes flew open, and she realized the ringing hadn't stopped. It wasn't a dream. Someone was outside, pressing her doorbell.

She glanced at the time on her bedside clock. It was after midnight. The only person who visited her at this hour was Jonas, and he had a key.

Or had he forgotten it?

It wouldn't be the first time.

Hoping he'd returned to stay the night, Sadie hopped out of bed, walked to the front door, and switched on the porch light, saying, "Jonas? Is that you?"

There was no response.

"Jonas?"

Still nothing.

She stood on her tiptoes, looking through the peephole. A man standing on the opposite side of the door smiled and waved. He was handsome in a polished kind of way in a tailored suit, and every strand of his blond hair was in place.

Through the door, she said, "Who are you, and why are you here?"

"Oh, hi," the man said. "Are you Sadie?"

Her heart picked up speed, a restless rhythm she couldn't control, betraying the calm she tried so hard to project.

Who was this guy?

"How do you know my name?" she asked.

"I'm Adam. I work with Jonas."

Jonas had mentioned his coworkers before, but never by name, and no one he knew had ever stopped by the condo before. Then again, Jonas had never asked her to watch a toddler before today, either.

"How do you know Jonas?" she asked.

"We work together at Prosperity Investments."

It explained his attire, but not why he was still dressed up so late at night. "Do you live around here?"

"Not far. I'm in Summerlin."

"Then you live over by Jonas."

It was a test.

Would he pass?

"He's about eight miles from me in Spring Valley," he said.

The first test had been passed, but still, her nerves refused to settle.

"Why are you here?" she asked. "It's late."

"I'm kind of embarrassed to say given the fact, you're ... well, his girlfriend. Anyway, Jonas was planning on stopping back by your place tonight, but he got held up with a work thing, so he asked me to do him a favor."

Figures.

"He always gets held up," she said. "It still doesn't explain why you're here."

"Oh, right. Jonas asked me to stop by and check in on Nora."

Heeding the warning Jonas had given her earlier in the day, she said, "Who's Nora?"

"I understand he ask you to protect her and not let anyone know she's here. I'm sure he told you she's the daughter of one of our most important clients."

"What if he did?"

"I hear the kid's been through a lot today. He asked me to grab a few things for her and drop them off for you."

She heard what sounded like plastic being jiggled around, and she brought her eye to the peephole once again. Adam waved a couple of bags in front of it, then reached in, pulling out a child's coloring book.

So far, everything the man said seemed legit.

Except, it was out of character for Jonas to send a stranger to her door without communicating with her about it first.

As if picking up on her trepidation, Adam said, "I'm not trying to cause any problems here."

"It's just, Jonas has never introduced me to any of his work colleagues before, and I don't know why he didn't tell me you were coming."

"I'm sure he meant to, but he hasn't had a spare second to himself since he got to work today. But yeah, I'm not surprised we haven't been introduced. I've worked with him for five years, and I still feel like there's a lot I don't know about him. To be honest, I didn't even know about you until today, and that's no disrespect on his part. He just likes keeping his work life and his private life separate."

Adam had a point.

Jonas was the most secretive, tight-lipped man she'd ever dated.

She slid the chain lock into place and then cracked open the door. "If the two of you don't know a lot about each other, why did he send you and not someone else?"

"He trusts me, and you know Jonas. He doesn't trust many people. He knows he can count on me when he's in a bind."

She'd often questioned whether Jonas trusted her, until today, when he'd shown up with the kid. The fact that he'd asked her to look after Nora instead of his wife made her feel special and validated, like the relationship they had was real.

Given the man didn't seem to pose a threat, Sadie unlocked the door, letting him inside.

He flashed her a calming smile as she did so.

"Thank you for helping Jonas out," she said. "It's nice of you. I've been stuck here all day with this kid."

"No problem. Where shall I set these bags?"

Sadie pointed toward the kitchen. "Anywhere on the counter is fine."

He set the bags down, then said, "How's Nora doing?"

"She's fine, I guess. She cried herself to sleep. Do you … umm, know anything about her or why she's here?"

"What has Jonas told you?"

"He said the kid's mother is dead."

Adam leaned against the kitchen counter and crossed his arms. "Did he tell you why?"

"Nora's mother was involved in something bad, I guess. He didn't say what it was, though, or why he's responsible for the kid. I thought her mother might have had a drug overdose. Do *you* know?"

He shrugged. "I don't."

"When he first brought her to me I assumed Nora was one of his relatives, maybe the daughter of a cousin or something.

The kid seems to know him, and he referred to himself as 'Uncle Jonas.' She's been mumbling stuff I don't understand most of the day, but earlier she pointed at a photo of him I'd stuck on the fridge, and she said 'Jo-Jo.'"

"Huh. Have you and Jonas been dating long?"

"Almost a year now. I'm surprised he told you about me."

"Why?"

"He never takes me out in public. Not around here, anyway. We take short trips together sometimes, but he's always worried about going into the city and being recognized. I think he's being ridiculous. Six hundred thousand people live here. What are the odds he'd be noticed?"

"Higher than you think. We have a lot of clients." Adam gestured to a chair in the living room. "Mind if I sit down?"

"Sure."

"I'm guessing the reason Jonas doesn't take you out has more to do than just his wife."

"What other reason is there?"

"It's the job. We work with a specific kind of client, and image—"

She lifted a finger. "Hold on. If you're going to say I don't look like the kind of woman he'd be with—don't. I may not be high class like his innocent, simple-minded wife, but I'm still classy."

"I didn't mean to say ... you're taking it all wrong. You're a beautiful woman, Sadie. I see why he likes you."

Charming *and* nice.

If things didn't work out with Jonas, Adam had definite potential.

"Do you have a special lady in your life?" she asked.

"I don't. It's easier to do my job without one."

She laughed. "Your job? Managing hedge funds?"

He smiled again. "Yes, well, I've kept you long enough. Would it be possible to look in on Nora before I go?"

"If you wake her, she'll start crying for her mother, and I'm exhausted. There's only so much I can take."

"I'll be quiet. I promise."

He didn't even know the child, so Sadie couldn't understand why it mattered so much, but she nodded anyway and headed for the stairs. She was about to head up when she turned around, freezing in place as she heard a distinct click, a familiar click, a sound taking her back to her childhood when she lived with her mother and two brothers in a trailer park on the wrong side of town.

She turned, her eyes locking on the gun pointed at her head. A silencer was attached to the end, and there was only one reason he'd take such a precaution.

As the tears began swimming in her eyes, she said, "I don't understand. What's going on?"

This time when he looked at her, his grin was shadowed by cold indifference. "I'm sorry, Sadie. You truly are a beautiful woman. I wish it didn't have to be this way, and if Jonas wouldn't have involved you, it wouldn't be."

23

R *aine*

Raine rested her head on Nora's pink, heart-shaped pillow, listening to the ticking of the moving hands on the princess clock on Nora's nightstand. It was almost three in the morning, and she hadn't slept a wink. Her mind stirred with questions about what had happened to Juliette and why, and what she may have been caught up in that led to her demise.

She heard footsteps shuffling down the hall, and she reached for her gun, relieved when Seth poked his head in and said, "Hey, Raine? You still awake?"

"Yeah, come on in."

It seemed neither of them would be getting any sleep tonight.

He walked into the room, switched on the lamp, and leaned against the wall. "Sorry to bother you. Are you sure you weren't sleeping?"

She shook her head.

"Me either," he said. "I've spent the last few hours going over everything we've learned so far. I'm sure you've done the same. One thing will come to mind, which leads to something else, which leads to all kinds of crazy thoughts and assumptions ..."

"I know what you mean. And hey, I want to apologize."

"For what?"

"I should have been honest with you from the start."

He shrugged it off. "Don't worry about it. It would have been nice if you had told me when I called, but I get why you didn't. We're all good now, right?"

"We're all good." Raine pushed the pillow behind her back and sat up. "Has thinking about things tonight helped in any way?"

He nodded. "Somewhere in all the jumbled-up chaos in my head, I remembered something."

"Oh, yeah? What?"

"About a week ago, I used Juliette's car to run errands. On my way back home, I thought I'd get her car washed and vacuumed. I was cleaning out the trash in the pocket of the driver's side door, and I found a wadded-up business card."

"A business card for ...?"

"A jeweler in the city."

"Did you ask Juliette about it?"

He shook his head. "Our anniversary is next month, and I convinced myself she'd bought something for me as a surprise. And since she took the time to crunch it up, I thought if I mentioned it to her, she'd either be mad at me for spoiling the surprise or think I was snooping around her vehicle, even though I wasn't."

"What did you do with the business card? Do you still have it?"

"I didn't see any reason to keep it, so I tossed it out. I remember the name on the card, though. Strand Jewelry Company."

Could the tennis bracelet have come from there?

Raine needed to know.

"I have an idea," she said.

"Go on."

"When the jewelry store opens, let's go there and see what we can find out."

24

M^{ax}

Inconvenient.

It was the perfect word to describe the last twenty-four hours of Max's life. He didn't *like* being inconvenienced. He didn't *accept* being inconvenienced. And yet, here he was, standing at the mini bar in his office at five in the morning, pouring a second glass of cognac as he mulled over the best way to continue cleaning up after the current fiasco.

Max had always avoided getting involved in the business end of things, which was why he'd hired others, handpicking the perfect men to do it for him. It was the reason he paid them so generously. He expected compliance without question, and he was used to getting it. Anything else wasn't tolerated.

He took a sip of cognac and thought of a quote his father had told him when he was just starting out in life, before he had the kind of money he had now. His father had said an organization was only as strong as its weakest link. If his father were still alive, he'd be proud to see all Max had achieved. At fifty-five, he'd made more than his father ever had in his lifetime.

Max didn't allow weak links, and right now, he had one.

A chink in the chain.

Where there was one, there would be more, which meant an example had to be made.

He finished the cognac and set the glass on the bar, rubbing a hand over his trimmed beard. Then he lifted a large, framed print of wild horses splashing through a river off the wall. Behind the print was a television. He switched it on. One large screen became six smaller screens, two rows of three—surveillance cameras he used to check up on a few of his most valued employees. He clicked a button in the top-right corner, and various angles of Jonas's house sparked to life.

He zoomed in, and he didn't like what he saw. He supposed he could call on one of his men to deal with it, but at this point, he'd grown weary of not getting the results he wanted. And even though he expected his men would do what needed to be done, most of them liked Jonas enough to make Max question their allegiance.

Taking Jonas down would require the best.

And in his mind, there was only one person for the job.

25

J onas

Over the past hour, Jonas had struggled with a dilemma: He needed to find a discreet way to warn Seth his life was in danger without giving away his involvement in Juliette's murder. When Max learned Jonas hadn't finished the assignment he'd been given, he'd send someone else, and Jonas doubted Seth even owned a firearm. Even if he did, Jonas doubted he knew how to use it. Weighing his options, he found a simple solution, and he acted on it.

Jonas cared for Seth, but he cared about the survival of his own family even more, so he made a decision. He'd grab Nora from Sadie, pick up his wife, and the three of them would start a new life somewhere they'd be untouchable by Max.

Telling his wife the truth about all that had happened would be difficult. She still believed he worked in hedge funds, not that he made his living as a killer for hire. Harder still would be explaining why they had to keep Nora, and why they could never go home. But once she understood, once she saw the danger they were all in, he was certain her love for him would outweigh it all.

Any other outcome was unthinkable.

Grabbing his cell phone, he made a call.

Come on, come on, pick up.

The phone rang five times and went to voicemail, and he wondered if she was still asleep. He sent a text message, urging her to call him as soon as she read it. Then he tried again.

This time, Anne's faint, tired voice answered. "Babe, what's going on? Is everything okay?"

"I'm sorry to wake you. How's your dad doing?"

"Good. He's glad I came to see him. Why are you calling so early?"

"I just wanted to hear your voice, honey. I miss you."

"Aww, you're so sweet. I'll be home soon. How's Seth? We've been following the story on the news. I tried calling him earlier. He didn't answer. As soon as I get home, let's have a conversation about what we can do for him."

Anne was unlike any woman he'd ever met. She was kind, loving, and more concerned about others than she was with herself. He thought about all the times he'd been unfaithful, wishing now he would have been the man she'd always deserved. He could be better, and he would be, for her and for Nora.

"Seth is struggling," he said. "It hasn't been easy for him. Juliette's sister is here, and it looks like she's staying with him for now. I'm sure having her around is helping."

"I'm glad to hear it."

"Listen, I was thinking ... it's been a while since we went away together. Why don't we have ourselves a little getaway?"

"Are you serious? Where are you thinking?"

"It's a surprise. You don't even have to come home first. I'll pack a bag for you, and I'll come to you."

"All right, sure. I can't wait."

"Me either. I'll see you soon."

Jonas ended the call, shoved his cell phone into his pocket, and rounded the corner into the living room, jumping back when he realized he wasn't alone.

"Max? How did you get in here?"

Max was sitting on the sofa, one leg crossed over the other, his hand resting on the gun on his lap. His demeanor was cool and controlled, like always, putting Jonas on edge. Over time he'd learned something about Max. The calmer Max was, the more cause there was for concern.

"Hello, Jonas," Max said. "Going somewhere?"

Jonas moved a hand to his hip, tensing when he realized his gun wasn't where it should have been. In his haste to get things moving, he'd placed it on the desk by the front door, intending to grab it when he left.

"After what happened yesterday, I decided I needed a break," Jonas said. "I assume you heard my phone call?"

"I hear *all* your phone calls. I see what goes on here too. Are you surprised?"

Jonas tore his gaze from Max and fixed it on the gun resting on the desk, which was seven, maybe eight feet away. Too far. If Max lifted his weapon, Jonas wouldn't make it there before Max had a chance to pull the trigger.

"What are you doing here?" Jonas asked.

Max placed a hand over the gun, patting it like it was a pet. "Do you know how much of an inconvenience it is for me to take care of things myself, to smooth over problems I pay *you* to resolve for me?"

"I know everything didn't go as planned yesterday, and I

apologize for that. You were right. I should have handled it myself. I thought we were going to talk about it when I stopped by this morning."

Max wagged a finger in the air, expressing his disapproval. "What happened to you, Jonas? You used to be the one man I could count on to get the job done. These past months, you seem to be self-destructing."

"I'm the same man I've always been. It's just, it was different this time. The others, I didn't know them on a personal level. They were just a job. With Juliette, it was different."

"It's a paycheck. Personal. Not personal. It shouldn't matter."

"It *does* matter, though. I cared for Juliette. I thought you did too."

"I cared for her a great deal, but this discussion isn't about her."

"How can it not be? Everything that's happening is because of her."

"I trained you, and all these years, I didn't just see you as someone who works for me. I saw you as family, until yesterday."

Jonas took a step toward the desk, a casual step he hoped wouldn't raise much suspicion, even though he was a fool to think Max hadn't expected it.

"I may not have handled things right with Juliette, but as hard as it was, and as much as I didn't want to do it, I still took care of her for you," Jonas said.

"*You* didn't take care of anything. You left her demise to Victor. You screwed up, putting all I've worked for in jeopardy."

"I never meant for it to blow back on you. It was a mistake, a lack in judgment. It won't happen again."

"You're right. It won't."

There was room for interpretation in Max's words, but Jonas assumed the worst. "What aren't you saying?"

Max looked him dead in the eye. "You don't think I keep tabs on your life? Your wife? Your family? Your whores? I must say, if I have to choose the one thing I'll miss the most, it will be watching your wife undress."

Max had been watching his wife.

When?

And how?

And then it came to him—*cameras.*

How stupid he'd been.

But where were they?

He'd suspected Max had been keeping an eye on him once before, but when he'd done a thorough check of the house, he found nothing. Now, he stood there, glancing around, assuming cameras had been hidden in just about every room of the house.

He thought of his wife.

Her privacy, *his* privacy, all violated.

Max wasn't there to talk.

He was there to kill him.

If Jonas had any chance for survival, he had to act—now. He leapt for his gun, but before he could reach it, Max issued a warning. "Unless you want to die in the next few seconds, *don't.*"

"Die in the next few seconds? As opposed to what—dying five minutes from now?"

Max fingered the gun in his hand, admiring it. "You know something? I love this gun. You gave it to me for my birthday a couple of years ago. Remember? So efficient. So ... quiet."

It was paradoxical, given the circumstances.

"Is that why you brought it? Is it one last lesson you want to teach me before you end my life?"

Jonas raised his hands in front of him. "We can fix every-thing. I'll help you. It can all return to normal again."

Max leaned forward. "You had it all, you know. Anne's a beautiful little thing. Charming and loving. One hell of a good cook from what I've seen. She's the kind of woman who makes a man want to clean up his act. Not you, though. You were never satisfied with one. You just had to have your side ornaments."

"Mock me all you like but leave my wife out of it."

"Why? You worried I'll kill her too? I won't, you know, not unless I have a reason."

"You'll never have a reason. If you've been watching like you say you have, then you know she doesn't know anything about my work life."

"I can't help but wonder what she'll say when I tell her the truth about who you are and what you've done. She'll be so disappointed to hear about Juliette. Even more to hear about your role in it all."

"I didn't kill Juliette."

Max threw his head back and laughed. "You didn't kill her? Oh, no. Of course you didn't. You just made sure the lamb made it to the slaughter."

"I did it for *you*! On *your* orders!"

"Whom will your wife believe if you're not around to defend yourself? I must say, the timing couldn't be better. The loss of one woman in my life has opened the door to other."

As the conversation went on, Jonas managed to move another foot, his gun almost within his reach.

He lunged for it again.

This time, Max fired.

The bullet hit Jonas in the chest, and he dropped to the floor. Max leapt off the couch and crouched down, hovering over Jonas, the pistol pressed against his head.

"Why do you think I sent Adam here last night? I had to

know what you'd done with Nora. Turns out, you stowed her away somewhere you shouldn't have."

As blood spilled out of the open wound, Jonas pressed a hand to his chest. Max reached into his pocket and pulled out his cell phone, shoving it in Jonas's face. "You aren't as clever as you think you are. It didn't take long for us to find out Nora was with your mistress. Your *dead* mistress. See for yourself."

Horrified, Jonas stared at Max's phone screen.

No.

It couldn't be ...

"See what I had to do," Max said. "This is *your* fault. It's *all* your fault."

Jonas jerked his head to the side. "I've seen enough, Max. Don't make me see what you did to Nora."

"What I did to Nora? You must think I'm an animal."

"Aren't you?"

"I wouldn't harm a hair on that child's precious head."

"Why is she so important to you? Why was she worth going after? Why kill the mother and keep the child?"

"If you were loyal, you wouldn't ask such questions. When you refused to bring her to me yesterday, it told me you questioned my judgment, and if you question my judgment, you can no longer be trusted."

"I've been nothing but loyal to you since the day we met."

Max jerked his head toward the hallway. "The bags you just packed suggest otherwise. You were leaving, Jonas. And you weren't coming back. Don't make me out to be a sucker."

"None of this would be happening if you wouldn't have killed Juliette for your own selfish reasons. She chose to run instead of staying with you, and you couldn't handle the fact that she didn't want to be with you anymore."

"You've got it all wrong. I couldn't allow her to leave because of what she saw. And yes, I cared for her, but it was her decision to leave, not mine. I did everything I could to keep her here, and it still wasn't enough. She knew the consequences."

"You say you won't harm Nora. Let's say I believe you. What will happen to her?"

"She's young. The life I will provide will be so lavish she won't remember anything that came before it. Her old life will fade away, replaced with a new story and new memories. It will be like all this never happened."

Jonas laughed. "You're fooling yourself, Max. She may not be young, but she'll never forget her mother."

As if to punctuate that truth, Jonas delivered a head-butt to Max's face. The gun sailed through the air. Jonas drew back a fist and then let it fly, Max's face the target. Max recoiled, and Jonas shoved Max out of his way, crawling toward his pistol.

Max went the opposite direction, spun around, and aimed, grunting, "Don't move, Jonas."

With his second failed attempt at retrieving his gun, he turned toward Max. "You're a sick man. A sick, twisted man."

Max screwed his face into a smile. "And you, my friend, are a dead one."

26

dam

Adam dropped Nora off at Max's house and then set out to do what he did best. He made a call and then listened to the instructions that followed. The subject for today was Mr. Richard Vanhorn, a wealthy casino owner. In recent months, he'd been carrying on an affair with the neighbor across the street, sneaking her over every Tuesday and Friday morning between six and seven while his wife, Eva, was at spin class.

Richard was convinced his wife suspected nothing. Adam knew better. If there was one thing he'd learned in his line of work, it was that women were almost always sharper than their husbands gave them credit for, and find out, she had.

Eva confirmed the liaison by doing a little surveillance of her own, and once she had proof, she had a decision to make.

When Eva married Richard years before, she'd signed a prenup. If he divorced her, she got next to nothing, and since she came from nothing, she wasn't about to go back to it, not after the lavish life she'd grown accustomed to over the years.

It was the kind of job Adam relished—double the victims, double the pay, half the recon work.

When he'd first met with Eva to discuss the details, he'd seen her vicious side firsthand, and though he had a strict policy of never dating a client, he found her hard to resist. But resist he did, though he wasn't sure he'd be able to a second time.

Adam parked a few blocks away, in the back corner of a grocery store lot where the security cameras only covered the first thirty feet past the entrance. He slipped out of the car disguised in a black wig, aviator shades, and a ball cap and hiked the distance to Richard's house, slipping through a side window Eva had left open for him. He removed his shoes, pausing a moment and then following the raucous voices he heard coming from the master bedroom.

Stepping inside, he found Richard and the neighbor tangled together on the bed, so lost in each other they hadn't even noticed him come in. Adam could have popped them both right then and there, called the cleaner, and been done with it. But he preferred a bit of conversation first, a healthy amount of build-up, leading to the main event.

"Hello," Adam said.

Richard turned, eyes wide.

The neighbor tried to scream, but before she got the chance, Adam silenced her with a single bullet to the center of her forehead, and she slinked down on the bed like a limp noodle.

Terrified, Richard tried to speak, but the panic attack he appeared to be having made it impossible.

"Take a breath, Richard," Adam said. "I don't need you having a heart attack on me."

"What ... in ... the ... who ... are ... you?"

Adam gave Richard a thumbs-up and said, "Hey, not bad. Way to use your words. Allow me to introduce myself. My name is Adam, and I'm sure you're wondering what I'm doing here and why I just shot your friend here. Am I right?"

Richard glared at Adam, saying nothing.

"Come on, now," Adam said. "I'm going to need you to participate in this conversation."

There was a long pause, and then Richard said, "Do I know you?"

"Good. I like that we're talking. To answer your question, no. You don't know me, but your wife does."

"My ... wife? Where is she? Is she all right?"

"You don't need to worry about Eva. She's just fine. Better than fine, in fact." Adam shot Richard a wink and continued. "I'm sure Eva's having the time of her life right now in spin class, thinking of all the ways she's going to spend your money once she takes control of the casino."

"What in the hell are you talking about?"

A faint noise outside the room caught Adam's attention, pulling him out of the lighthearted rhythm of the banter they'd been having. He froze, listening, then glanced at the bedroom door, his smile fading while he mulled over what, or who, might be out there.

He didn't appreciate distractions.

The Vanhorn's had no children and no pets, and Adam had been assured it was uncommon for anyone to stop by at this hour. Even so, someone or some*thing* was in the hallway. In order to find out, he'd have to step into out of the room, and that wasn't something he was willing to do.

Adam backed against the wall, giving himself a full view of Richard and the door, and then he raised the gun at the man's head and whispered, "Hate to cut this short, but it seems things have taken a turn."

Before he could pull the trigger, Eva entered the room, offering Adam a wry grin. "Don't rush out on my account. Stay awhile."

Adam clenched his jaw, irritation flashing across his face. Eva had ignored his instructions, a direct violation of the contract she'd signed. She supposed to stay out of it, let him handle everything, and stay away until she received word she could return home again. But here she was, standing in the middle of it all, unfazed, and grinning like a child on Christmas morning.

"Ma'am, we talked about this, and we agreed," Adam said. "You can't be here."

She swished a lock of her long, blond hair out of her face and batted her large blue eyes at him. "Of course I can be here. It's fine. I mean, some rules are meant to be broken, right? Besides, I tried to stay away. Let's just say I couldn't resist."

"It's important for my jobs to go as planned. That's what makes me good at what I do."

Eva ignored the comment and glanced at the bed. "One down, and one to go, I see. Oh, hello Richard."

"Eva, honey, what have you done?"

"I did what I had to do, *honey*, but I can explain if you'd like."

Richard looked down as if just realizing he was still on his knees, naked. He reached for the sheet, attempting to cover himself, and in doing so, the neighbor's body shifted, flicking blood onto his arm. He shrieked, flicking it off as he began sobbing.

"I'm aware of the affair you've been having with the neighbor," Eva said. "I've known for some time. I suppose you think I'm an idiot, that your affair could keep going on, and you'd just get away with it. Did you think the smell of her odious perfume wouldn't linger once she'd gone?"

"Eva," Adam said. "I have a job to do."

"I'm aware. I just have a favor to ask. I was hoping I could .. you know ..." She held a hand out. "Might I finish him off myself?"

There was something intoxicating about the idea of her pulling the trigger. It stirred something in him. Still, he couldn't let it happen.

"I'm afraid not," he said.

"Ahh, well. It was worth a try. Quick and painless, please, just like we discussed."

Adam steadied his breathing, trying to refocus, a task that didn't come easy. He nodded at Eva, aimed, and fired a single shot. Richard's body slumped over his mistress, and just like that, it was all over.

Eva took a step toward the bed, and Adam was quick to stop her.

"Don't," he said. "You could contaminate the scene and incriminate yourself."

"I could just say I came in and they were already dead."

"Please," Adam said. "I need you to do exactly what we discussed. Now, let's get out of here. The cleaner's on his way."

She sauntered toward Adam with the ease of a woman who knew every eye would follow her in a crowded bar. When she reached him, she pressed her lips to his and murmured, "What can I do to thank you?"

"I've been paid. It's thanks enough."

Pressing a hand against his crotch, she said, "What if I want to leave a tip?"

Never before had Adam been so attracted to a woman. And for the first time, he found the idea of the two of them in bed together impossible to resist.

Adam checked the time. His next appointment wasn't for a

couple of hours. Grabbing her hand, he said, "You can thank me, but not here," and a thought crossed his mind—Maybe it was time he broke a few rules himself.

27

R *aine*

Raine dried off with a towel, put a track suit on, and opened the bathroom door. The hall was quiet and empty, and she saw no sign of Seth. Hoping to speak to him about the plans they'd made to visit the jeweler, she said, "Seth, are you there?"

He didn't answer.

"Seth, can you hear me?"

Still nothing.

She walked to the living room. The television was still on, but Seth wasn't there. Earlier he'd said something about heating up a couple breakfast burritos before they left, so she checked the kitchen. He wasn't there. She searched the house, going from room to room before it occurred to her he might have left, perhaps deciding to speak to the jeweler on his own. But when she pushed the kitchen curtains aside, his car was still in the driveway.

So where was he?

As she passed the kitchen again, something caught her eye. She stopped and leaned toward the window. Outside, in the back yard, an elongated shadow stretched along the fence—still, silent, and out of place.

She grabbed her gun and slid the back door open, making it a few steps outside when she heard, "Pssst."

Lowering her gun, she breathed a sigh of relief.

"I've been looking all over for you," she said.

He lifted a finger to his lips as if suggesting she keep quiet.

"What's going on?" she asked.

"I was outside a few minutes ago, filling the pool, and I saw a man coming out of Jonas's house."

Raine shrugged. "Maybe he has company."

"I don't think so. This guy was dressed in all black, and he looked like he was taking every precaution to make sure he wasn't seen."

Thinking Seth waws being a bit dramatic, Raine said, "What do you mean?"

"The man looked both ways, then crouched low and slipped toward the back gate before vaulting over it like a gymnast. I don't know. Something doesn't feel right. I should walk over and make sure Jonas is all right."

"Good idea. I'll come with you."

Seth glanced at her wet hair and shook his head. "The jewelry place opens in thirty minutes. Why don't you keep getting ready, and I'll go check things out. I'm sure it's nothing. Jonas is the toughest guy I know."

Not wanting him to go over alone, she hesitated, but then said, "Yeah, okay."

Less than a minute later, she regretted the decision, slipping her sandals on as she headed for the front door. As soon as she swung it open, she saw Seth standing in front of her, his pants stained with what appeared to be blood.

Shocked, she said, "What happened? Are you bleeding?"

He looked down. "I'm ... no ... it's not mine ... not my blood."

"Has something happened to Jonas?"

Seth stared at Raine, eyes wide, body trembling.

"Seth, talk to me," Raine said. "Where is Jonas?"

Seth reached for her hand, yanking her onto the porch. "I need to ... need to show you ..."

"Need to show me what?"

"Come with me. Right now."

28

Jonas lay sprawled across the living-room floor, face up, eyes closed as if he was sleeping. But the pool of blood spreading beneath him told another story. Raine stepped closer, scanning his body. There were two gunshot wounds, one to the head and another to the chest.

The metallic scent of blood filled the air, and Raine looked around. She spotted a gun on the ground several inches from his right hand, as though it had slipped from his grasp in his final moment. She knelt and checked his pulse, even though she'd seen enough dead people in her day to know one when she saw one.

Seth sank onto the couch, his head in his hands, rocking back and forth. "I don't understand. First my wife, and then my daughter goes missing, and now Jonas. Why? Why is this happening?"

"Seth, did you call 9-1-1 before you came to get me?"

His breath was fast and heavy, and he was mumbling something too low for her to hear.

"Seth, you'll pass out if you don't slow down," Raine said.

"Take a few breaths and listen to me, okay? Did you call for an ambulance or for the police?"

"I, umm, I didn't have my phone on me. It's at the house. I could go back get it."

"You stay put. I'll make the call."

Raine pulled her phone from her back pocket, dialed 9-1-1, gave the address, and described the scene around her. The operator asked her to stay on the line, but she hung up. Time was a precious commodity, and at present, she didn't have a lot of it.

Raine canvassed the room, her eyes flashing from object to object, looking for anything to explain who had been here, what had happened, and why. The most straightforward cause of death was suicide. Or a scene that was made to look like a suicide. But after meeting Jonas the night before, Raine didn't believe he was the type to take his own life.

Often when men committed suicide, they were quick and efficient. It wouldn't have made sense for Jonas to have shot himself in two different places when a single bullet to the head could have done the job. She also found it odd that he would kill himself less than twenty-four hours after suggesting Juliette had done the same.

The chest wound he'd sustained was off-center, too far to the right to have been the killing blow. The headshot, though, was precise, killing him in an instant.

She walked around the room and found a piece of paper folded in half on a small table in the entryway. It seemed convenient. Almost *too* convenient.

The words *Las Vegas Metro Police Department* were printed across the front in bold type. Her pulse quickened. Using the cuff of her shirt to keep from smudging it with fingerprints, she slid the fabric beneath the fold and pried the envelope open.

Inside was what appeared to be a suicide note.

· · ·

For a while now, I've been having an extramarital affair with Juliette Granger. Two days ago, she ended the relationship. She said she was leaving her husband, and she was also leaving me. I woke up yesterday morning, saw her pulling out of the driveway, and I knew she was taking off for good. I went after her. I caught up to her in the Virgin River Gorge, and I tried to get her to pull over so we could talk. She refused to put her window down, and when my car got too close to hers, she lost control and went over the edge.

I pulled over at the next exit and hiked down to the car. It was then I realized Nora was inside. It looked like she was still breathing. I shattered the window in the back seat and pulled her out. A few minutes later, she died in my arms.

Not wanting Seth to see his daughter battered and broken, I made the decision to take her to a place Juliette told me was one of her favorite spots, and I buried her there, something I felt I had to do. I couldn't bear the thought of Seth or anyone else who loved her seeing the way she was at the end.

In the hours that followed, I knew I couldn't live with the guilt of what I've done. To Seth and my wife Anne, I can't tell you how sorry I am. I didn't mean for it to end this way. I hope one day you can forgive me.

What happened was an accident. I never meant for them to die. I loved them. I loved them both.

. . .

—Jonas

Raine turned toward Seth who was still on the couch, shoulders sagging, mourning the man he thought he knew. In a matter of minutes, his grief would turn into something darker. She looked down at the note, searching for the right words and finding none. She wanted to protect him from what it said, but the police were on their way, and it was better he heard it now, with her by his side.

She sat next to him on the couch, and he looked up at her. "What's wrong?"

"Jonas left a note. You better read it."

"What does it say?"

Attempting to be a pillar for them both, Raine choked back the tears. "It's not good, Seth. I'm sorry. And it's not going to be easy for you to read, but I think it's best you do before the police arrive."

She held the note out to him. Seth hesitated before taking it, his fingers trembling as he unfolded the paper. His eyes moved slowly down the page, and with each line, the color drained from his face a little more.

By the time he reached the end, his expression had hardened into something between disbelief and devastation. He sat in silence for several seconds, the weight of it settling in, and she knew the stillness wouldn't last.

"No, No! No! No! No! No!" he yelled. "This doesn't make any sense. Jonas was my friend. He wouldn't do this to me. He wouldn't hurt me this way. He wouldn't hurt my family. I would have known if something was going on between them. There's no way any of this is true. No flipping way!"

Seth grabbed a lamp off a side table, hurling it against the wall. The porcelain base shattered, sending jagged fragments in all directions. The cops wouldn't be pleased, but Raine wasn't about to rob him of his anger.

An ambulance and a couple of squad cars pulled into the driveway, and Raine pulled out her phone, making a quick call while she still had the chance.

"Detective Ford? It's Raine. My sister's neighbor is dead. He left a written confession, admitting to her murder and to Nora's. Sheriff Sanders, a few police officers, and an ambulance just pulled up, but you need to be here. You need to see this for yourself."

29

Two hours later, Raine was in Seth's kitchen making him and Ford a cup of coffee. Seth wasn't talking, which wasn't a surprise. Over the last couple of hours, he'd only said the bare minimum.

She set the coffees on the table and sat down, noticing the blank look on Seth's face as he wrapped his hands around his cup. She couldn't fault him for it. Grief had a way of hollowing a person out, leaving only the shell. She'd managed to keep her own emotions under control, but the pressure was building. One wrong word, one flicker of a memory, and she knew she'd lose it.

Ford thanked her for the coffee and took a hearty swig. "I know you're not in the mood to talk right now, Seth, but if you could answer just a few for me, I'd appreciate it."

"I don't know what the answer to anything is anymore," Seth muttered. "Two days ago, I had a wife I thought I knew and a friend I thought I could count on. Today, they're strangers to me. I'm a chump. A blind idiot."

"You're being too hard on yourself. What they did isn't your fault, and the note Jonas left doesn't prove anything yet. Maybe he wrote it. Maybe he didn't."

Seth slid the coffee cup to the side. "Don't you get it? I no longer care."

A tear splashed down his cheek, and he flicked it away.

"I'm doing everything I can to piece everything together," Ford said. "And I won't stop until I do."

Seth shook his head. "Yeah, you will, because it's *over* now. It doesn't matter what evidence you collect or how long it takes to process. You have a signed confession. Jonas killed my wife and my child. There's nothing left to do except figure out where he buried my daughter."

"Jonas mentioned your daughter had a favorite place. Any idea what he's taking about?"

"I don't know, man."

"What about you?" Ford asked, turning toward Raine.

"I don't know, either. I need some time to think on it."

Ford nodded and placed a hand on Seth's shoulder. "I understand you're grieving, but don't presume this is the end of the investigation. Think about it. We have a gun with the serial numbers scratched out. And then there's the note. He admitted to burying Nora, but he never says where. Maybe he didn't want you to see her, but since he confessed to everything else, why not tell the police where to find her? Why not give you closure?"

Seth pushed his chair back and stood. "I need a break. I just ... I can't talk about any of this anymore. I can't answer your questions or anyone else's questions. I'm done."

He grabbed his car keys out of a bowl and headed out of the room.

"Where are you going?" Raine asked.

"For a drive. I can't be here."

"Seth, wait," she said. "Don't leave. You're not in the right frame of mind. Ford is right. We don't have all the facts yet.

Nothing has been proven. We don't know if there's any truth to what Jonas wrote. What if it isn't true? What if Nora is still alive? I'm not willing to give up until I'm certain."

Seth shook his head. "You know what I think? I think Juliette left me the way she did because she couldn't look me in the eye and tell me what she'd done. She lied to me, and she lied to you. She was a coward, Raine. She took the coward's way out, and she died for it."

Raine had every intention of responding until she looked at Ford whose expression prompted her to leave it alone, to let Seth go. She didn't want to, but she did.

Seth walked out the front door, at it slammed closed behind him.

Raine poured herself another cup of coffee and rejoined Ford at the table. "I understand what Seth's going through. And even though I wasn't as close as I could have been with my sister in recent months, I thought I knew her better."

"Hard to say how much truth there is to any of it. Take your neighbor, for example. He has two bullet wounds, one in the chest, one in the head. Now, I could take a guess and say he shot himself in the chest intending to end his life, and when that didn't work, he tried a second time. But something about the whole scenario seems off to me."

"Do you have any other theories?"

He swallowed back a sip of coffee and leaned toward her. "You're the medical examiner. *Do you?*"

She did.

"The way I see it, there are two possibilities," she said. "Jonas either committed suicide like the note suggests, or he was murdered. Let's say my sister was having an affair with Jonas and decided to run away from her problems. It still doesn't explain the bag full of money and where it came from."

"Good point."

"And why move to Colorado when she had me in Utah? It's extreme. Too extreme. She could have told me the truth and sought refuge at my house. So why didn't she? Whenever she was in a jam, I was there for her. Sure, Jonas said he ran her off the road like a jealous maniac. I met him yesterday, and he fits the jealous-maniac type. But I still find it hard to believe he committed suicide."

Ford twisted the coffee cup around in his hand. "Sheriff Sanders has spoken with Detective Whitaker of the Las Vegas Police Department, and he has agreed to work with me on the investigation. We're sending over everything we know so far from our department, even though we don't know much. We're still waiting on the forensics results from the car crash to come back. In the meantime, Sanders has ordered a search warrant for Jonas's place. Bet he'll get one for Seth's place too."

"I figured as much."

He wagged a finger at her. "You've had plenty of time to snoop around this place, and I'm assuming you did. Find anything?"

"I found several slinky cocktail dresses tucked inside one of her suitcases in the closet. Seth said he'd never seen them before, which means if they were hers—and they were her size, so I'm guessing they were—she must've worn them for someone else. What struck me most was that they weren't her style. I never saw her dress like that."

"With Seth out of town for work half the week, your sister spent a lot of time here alone. Maybe you're right, and she had another man in her life, whether it was Jonas or someone else. I've seen it before. People get tired of routine, of the same version of themselves day after day. Sometimes they just want an escape, a place where they can be someone else for a while."

"Makes sense to me."

"Back to those skimpy dresses. Suppose it wouldn't hurt to conduct some DNA testing on them. You find anything else?"

"There was a tennis bracelet inside a pocket of one of the dresses. I showed it to Seth, and he said he'd seen her wear it before, but she said I bought it for her, and I didn't. Then, about a week ago, Seth found a business card for a jeweler in Juliette's car. I'm thinking it might be where the bracelet came from."

"Can I see the bracelet?"

Raine nodded and walked to the bedroom, retrieving it for him. Handing it off, she said, "It looks a lot more expensive than what they can afford, and I don't think she would have bought something this extravagant for herself. I'm guessing it was a gift."

"What kind of money does Seth make?"

"Less than a hundred thousand a year."

"And your sister?"

"She hasn't worked since she had Nora."

Ford downed the rest of his coffee, and Raine grabbed their empty cups off the table, taking them to the sink.

"The dresses, the bracelet, and jeweler's card Seth found might be nothing, but I think we're on to something here," Ford said. "This entire case is troubling me. No matter what the letter we found says, my gut's telling me we're not finished with this case yet."

"I feel the same way."

Ford stood, walking over to Raine and givingher hand a gentle squeeze. "I'm sorry for all you're going through."

The tears were coming.

She could feel it.

And this time, she let them.

Ford remained quiet, wrapping his arms around the emotions that were pouring out of her.

A few minutes passed, and then he said, "It's going to be all right. I know it doesn't seem like it now, but it will be."

It wouldn't change anything, though.

No matter what else they discovered, her sister was gone, and so was her niece. She wanted to believe Nora was still out there, alive and waiting to be found. But she was logical enough to know the odds weren't on her side.

"Now that I've told you about the jeweler, are you planning on stopping by?" Raine asked.

"Right after I leave here. Why?"

"I'd like to come with you."

He crossed the room without answering and opened the front door, turning back to say, "I think it's best I speak to them first."

"I'd rather be there, to hear what they have to say."

Raine braced herself for the "no," but instead he tipped his head to the side and said, "Okay, fine. Let's get going."

30

Strand Jewelry was the kind of place a woman could lose track of time in and still not see everything the store had to offer. The glamorous establishment stretched across three glittering floors. Glass display cases lined with velvet showcased everything from vintage heirlooms to modern masterpieces, all beneath the soft glow of crystal chandeliers.

Six women moved around the main-level sales floor, each one dressed in a crisp ivory suit that matched the store's refined aesthetic. Their hair was pulled back into tight, polished buns that gave them an air of precision and poise.

Ford and Raine approached a pint-sized salesperson standing behind a counter where women's wedding rings were on display, and Ford asked to speak to the manager. The salesperson nodded, disappearing into a back room.

A few minutes later, she returned, walking beside a silver-haired man dressed in a dark tailored suit paired with a cream dress shirt and large diamond-stud earrings.

He approached and stuck out his hand. "Hello, I'm Nelson. You asked to speak with me?"

Ford nodded. "I'm Ford, and this is Raine. Is there somewhere we could speak in private?"

"Sure, follow me."

Nelson escorted them into one of the offices, offering them a bottle of sparkling water as they sat down. Then he sat at a desk, joining them.

"What can I do for you both?" he asked.

Raine reached into her pocket, pulled out the tennis bracelet, and showed it to him. "I was wondering if this bracelet came from here?"

Nelson leaned in for a closer look. "May I?"

She nodded and handed it to him.

After studying it for a moment, he said, "It's a fine piece, but it's not one of ours."

Raine leaned back, breathing a sigh of disappointment. "I was hoping you'd recognize it."

"Why do you think the bracelet came from here?"

"Your business card was found in my sister's car."

"Why don't you ask her where she got it?"

She bit her lip.

Keep it together, Raine

"I can't," she said. "My sister is dead."

His eyes widened. "Oh, my. I'm sorry."

"I noticed your store is spread out on three floors," Ford said. "Do you sell jewelry on all of them?"

"New jewelry is sold on the main level. Resale items are on the second, and the third floor is for repairs."

"When you say *resale*, do you mean consignment?"

"I do. We purchase high-end pieces from our customers and resell them."

Raine reached for her cell phone inside her purse and flipped through her photos until she found one of Juliette, which she showed to him. "Have you ever bought or sold jewelry to this woman?"

Nelson's attempt at keeping his composure seemed to fail the moment his eyes landed on the photo. He tried to mask it with a casual glance, but the quick flicker of recognition across his face said otherwise.

He *had* seen her before.

There was no doubt about it.

Studying Nelson's reaction, Ford seemed to catch it too.

"I ... let's see," Nelson said. "She looks familiar, but even if we'd met, we don't discuss our clients."

Based on the look on his face, the comment didn't sit well with Ford.

"Like Raine just said, her sister is dead," he said. "There's no need to protect her privacy anymore."

"Even so, there's not much I can tell you."

Ford tossed his badge onto the desk. "What about now?"

Nelson leaned back in his chair, tapping a finger to his lips.

He looked nervous.

Raine wondered why.

Glancing over at her, Nelson said, "What was your sister's name?"

"Juliette Granger."

He repeated the name a few times. "Wait a minute. Are you talking about the woman who died in the awful car accident in the Virgin River Gorge?"

"I am."

"Have you done business with her or not?" Ford pressed.

Nelson lowered his voice to a whisper. "Even though she's deceased, I shouldn't say anything. It's ... well, trust me when I say it's for the best. Besides, it's like I already told you. The bracelet isn't one of ours."

He was hiding something.

Raine was sure of it.

And she wasn't leaving until she got it out of him.

"We have reason to believe my sister's accident wasn't an accident," Raine said.

Nelson jerked his head back. "What are you saying?"

"I'm saying, she may have been murdered. Whatever you're holding back, and you *are* holding something back, we need to hear it."

Nelson remained still for a moment, and then he bolted out of his chair, rushed to the office door, and closed it. Returning to his desk, he said, "I don't understand. Why do you think she was murdered?"

"I can't go into that," Fold said. "If Juliette bought or sold anything to you, now's the time to speak up. I'd rather not make a scene, but if you keep evading me, I will."

Nelson nodded, taking a deep breath in. "All right, fine. I met with Juliette several days ago."

"I need the exact date and time," Ford said.

Nelson gave it to him, and then added, "She brought in a handful of pieces she wanted to sell. And I must say, they were impressive, all high-end."

"Did she mention where the jewelry came from or why she'd decided to sell them?" Raine asked.

"We don't ask personal questions. Although now that you mention it, I recall her saying she had far too much jewelry and was looking to offload some of it. But most of the pieces she brought in were newer, so I was surprised she'd decided to part with them so soon."

"What did she sell to you?"

"Now, let's see." He turned toward the computer, typed in a few things on the keyboard, and pulled up an invoice. "She brought in a watch, several pairs of earrings, a necklace, and a bracelet."

"How much did you pay her?"

"According to this invoice, we gave her a check for sixty-eight thousand dollars."

Ford and Raine exchanged glances, pleased at least one of their burning questions had been answered. The money in Juliette's duffel bag must have come from the jewelry she'd sold.

But who had bought her the jewelry?

Jonas?

"Did Juliette ever mention where the pieces came from?" Ford asked.

Nelson shook his head.

"I hope for your sake you're telling me the truth," Ford said.

"I am, I swear," Nelson said. "I held back before because we pride ourselves in the privacy we offer to our customers. But then you showed me your badge and told me she was dead ... and, well, that changed everything."

Ford looked at Raine. "I believe we're done here."

He handed his card to Nelson, telling him to give him a call if anything else about Juliette came to mind.

They were just about to the door when Nelson said, "Hold on a moment. After what you just shared with me, there's one more thing I should say."

"What is it?" Ford asked.

"When I met with Juliette, it was obvious she was going through a hard time."

"How do you know?" Raine asked.

"She was jumpy the day she came in. She looked worried and nervous. You could see it in the way she kept wringing her hands and glancing at the door, like she was expecting someone to walk in. Her phone rang once, and she nearly jumped out of her chair. I asked if everything was okay, and she broke down crying. I handed her a tissue, and she apologized for her behavior. I told her there was no need. After she left, I remember thinking she must have been going through a divorce or a breakup of some kind. Whatever it was, she was on edge, like she was carrying around the weight of something she couldn't shake."

31

"Ford and I just stopped by Strand Jewelry," Raine said, waiting to hear Seth's response.

He didn't say anything, but she could hear him breathing on the other end of the line—slow, sharp, and heavy —like he was angry.

"Did you hear me?" Raine asked.

"Yep."

"Don't you want to know what I found out?"

"Nope."

"Why not?"

"I thought we were supposed to go together. Why'd you go without me?"

"I'm sorry. When we spoke last, you made it clear you didn't want to discuss Juliette or what happened anymore, so I didn't think you still wanted to go. Look, we're just trying to get some answers."

Raine heard a click, and the line went dead.

She dialed his number again.

He didn't answer.

She tried once more, and he answered, but he didn't speak.

"Seth, don't hang up," she said. "Hear me out, all right?"

There was a long pause, and then he said. "Fine."

Raine told him everything that had transpired in their meeting with Nelson. When she finished, he said, "Well, isn't that just fantastic? I guess what Jonas said was true after all. I bet he gave her the bracelet and all those other things she sold. He made good money. I'm sure he could afford it."

"Nelson said she received a call while she was at the jewelry store, and that she was jumpy and on edge the entire time she was there. She even started crying. I'm wondering if Juliette may have tried to end things with Jonas, and he didn't accept it, and turned violent."

"I don't even know if I care anymore."

He sounded defeated and numb, which worried her.

"When will you be home?" she asked.

"Soon," he said, and he ended the call.

32

On the drive home, Raine pressed Ford for information.

"I wish we knew who called my sister when she was at the jewelry store," she said. "Have you looked through her phone records yet?"

"Yep, and there wasn't anything out of the ordinary. And before you ask, after we discovered Jonas this morning, I had one of my officers look to see if there were calls between them."

"And?"

"There weren't. Juliette made calls to you, to Seth, to a couple of her friends, and that's about it."

"I wonder what you'll find when you look at Jonas's records."

"Interesting you bring that up."

"Interesting, why?"

"Last I checked, the Las Vegas police haven't located his phone."

"It's weird, right?"

"I'd say so. You'd think it would have been in his pocket or beside his keys, or somewhere else in the house that makes sense, but so far, nothing."

It was odd.

"If Juliette and Jonas were having an affair, wouldn't you assume she called him from time to time, even if they lived next to each other?" Raine asked.

"If they were keeping their love affair a secret, maybe they made a rule not to communicate that way. Maybe they found an alternate form of communication."

"Like a burner phone?"

"Could be. If they *were* having an affair, they did a darn good job of keeping it quiet."

Raine and Ford pulled into the driveway in front of Seth's house just as the mailman was about to drop a stack of envelopes into the box. The man paused, frowning. Instead of inserting the mail, he reached inside and withdrew a single white envelope that was already there. He studied it with mild curiosity, turning it over in his hands.

Ford climbed out of the truck and walked toward him. "Something wrong?"

"Not sure," the mailman said. "Found this inside the box. It's addressed to Seth, but it doesn't have a stamp or postmark. Looks like someone put it here."

Ford held out his hand, and the mailman passed the envelope over. It was unsealed and handwritten, the kind of thing that raised alarms. Raine joined him at the curb, and for a long moment, the two of them stared at the envelope.

"What do you think?" Raine asked.

Ford's jaw tightened. "I think we'd better see what's inside."

They thanked the mailman, then headed into the house. Ford grabbed a pair of gloves from his truck and joined Raine in the living room. Using caution, he slid the envelope open, pulling out a folded piece of paper inside. The writing was smudged, like the note had been written in haste.

Raine leaned in close, her breath catching as she read over his shoulder:

Seth,

If you're reading this, you and Raine are in immediate danger. I wish I could say more, but I can't. What happened to Juliette wasn't an accident. If you stay here, the people who went after her will come for the two of you next.

If you ever trusted me, trust me now, and leave while you still can. Go away for a while and don't come back.

I'm sorry I wasn't a better friend, but if this reaches you in time, maybe it will save your life.

Jonas

Raine gasped, staring at the note, then at Ford. "I don't understand why Jonas would leave something like this if it wasn't true. He wouldn't risk it, not for nothing."

Ford's gaze hardened as he folded the letter and slid it back into the envelope. "I don't either. But if his warning is real, we may already a step behind."

She looked at him, fear flickering in her eyes. "You think someone's out there, watching us?"

"We can't rule it out," he said, scanning out the window. "If someone is coming, I'm not letting you out of my sight. Not for a second."

33

S *eth*

Seth couldn't remember the last time he'd sat in a bar alone.

Five years?

Longer?

He'd never been much of a drinker.

But today he drank.

As he knocked back his fourth beer, he wondered how many more it would take before he was able to detach from life altogether.

So far it wasn't working.

He considered leaving the bar, grabbing a twelve-pack at a convenience store and finishing in the privacy of his own home. But Raine might be there, and he didn't need her judgement. He didn't need to hear any more of her theories, either.

She may have still been looking for answers.

But he wasn't.

He'd accepted Juliette and Jonas were having an affair, and that it had cost them and him everything they ever cared about. And he was no longer interested in hearing what may have transpired between them. Raine could stay another day, maybe two. But then she needed to go.

He held a finger in the air, signaling the bartender. "Another."

The bartender removed the glass he'd just emptied and replaced it with a fresh one. As Seth brought it to his lips, his cell phone lit up.

Raine was calling.

Again.

If he didn't answer, he knew she'd keep calling, so he did what he should have done in the first place—he switched the phone off.

Over the past day, he'd started to realize just how hard it was for him to look at Raine. When he did, he saw Juliette. Sure, Raine's personality was different, but her mannerisms were the same. Her upper lip curved up when she talked, just like Juliette's had. She tipped her head to the right, just like Juliette, and from behind, their long hair and slim body shape were so similar, it was hard to tell them apart.

Seth remembered a time several years back when he'd grabbed Raine's waist and given it a squeeze. She turned around and he realized he'd squeezed the wrong sister.

Back then, he thought he had everything he'd ever wanted in life.

But now ... what did he have to live for when everything he cared for in life had been taken from him?

34

R *aine*

Seth was no longer answering Raine's calls. He still wasn't home, and it had been several hours since he stormed out. She considered he may have been avoiding her because he no longer wanted her around.

She didn't blame him.

But he was in danger, or so Jonas said.

Raine thought back to the first time she met Seth. Juliette had invited her over for dinner, and she'd assumed it would be just the two of them. Instead, when the door opened, there was Seth. He smiled, extended his hand, and introduced himself as Juliette's fiancé.

Raine was in shock.

Juliette appeared behind him, glowing as she flashed her the ring on her finger. She started talking about venues and colors and how they'd set a wedding date for three months from then.

Three short months.

She remembered standing there, trying to smile, to match her sister's excitement, but inside she was thinking: *Three months? I don't even know this guy. How well could she?*

It felt rushed, like a decision made on impulse, and she struggled to see how they could have been in love without knowing each other better.

Over time, she began to soften, seeing Seth from a different perspective as a doting husband and then a father. She thought Juliette was happy, or happy enough, and then the call came, and Juliette told Raine she was leaving him. None of it made sense, and now she knew why.

Next door, a woman stood in her front yard, speaking to a couple of police officers. Her arms were folded, and she was crying, her eyes a continuous fountain of tears. She brushed them away with her hand, wiping them on a cardigan she wore over a blue, knee-length dress.

One of the officers wouldn't stop talking, while the other kept looking around. She wished she knew what they were talking about. Several minutes passed, and the officer who'd done most of the talking placed a hand on the woman's shoulder. He said a few more things, and she bowed her head and nodded. Then they left.

The woman took her phone out of her pocket and made a call. Then she walked toward the house, but she didn't go inside. Instead, she spun around, glanced in Raine's direction, and walked over.

As Raine opened the door, the woman attempted a slight smile, saying, "Hi, I'm Anne."

"Nice to meet you. I'm Raine."

"Is Seth here?"

"He isn't."

She frowned. "Do you know when he'll be back?"

"I don't. I've been calling him for the past couple of hours. He won't answer my calls."

"He isn't answering mine, either. I heard you were with Seth when he found my husband, which makes you Juliette's sister. You look a lot like her."

Raine swung the door open. "Would you like to come in?"

"Sure."

As Raine closed the door, she looked around, then across the street at Ford, who was sitting in an unmarked car with Detective Whitaker. He nodded as if to put her at ease, to assure her everything was okay.

But was it?

Anne followed Raine to the living room, and Raine sat down. Anne remained standing, her hands fisted at her sides.

"I know we don't know each other, but I feel like if I don't get a few things off my chest, I'm going to lose it," she said. "It's just, I don't feel like it's right to unload everything on you when you lost someone too."

"Oh, I don't know. A vent session might be just what the two of us need right now."

Anne nodded and threw her hands in the air. "I don't understand what's going on."

"I feel the same way."

"I talked to Jonas this morning. He seemed stressed, like something was wrong, and then out of nowhere, he said he wanted us to go on a trip together, leaving today. It's just ludicrous. Juliette went off the road, which appeared to be an accident at first. And now, I'm supposed to believe my husband was having an affair with her?"

"It's a lot to take in."

"Why would my husband suggest we take a vacation and then kill himself less than an hour later? And then admitting to burying Nora? I can't get my head around it. Everything I've been told makes me feel the police are talking about someone else—not my husband."

"I don't want to believe it's true either. I've tried finding another explanation, but so far, there isn't one. In the note, he said something about burying her in a place that meant something to her. Any idea where?"

"None." Anne began pacing, her voice becoming more and more strained the more she talked. "Jonas loved Nora. I can't believe he would bury her and not give the location. He wouldn't commit suicide. I can't believe it. I won't."

Her body swayed from side to side, like a fragile flower caught in the wind. Then her eyes rolled back. Raine shot up from the sofa, reaching out just in time to keep her from hitting the floor. Her body collapsed into Raine's arms, and she knelt, lowering her onto the rug.

Anne appeared to be unconscious, but she was still breathing. Raine raised her legs, attempting to recall blood flow. She waited several seconds, but there was no change, and she reached for her phone to call Ford. Before she had the chance, Anne' eyes flashed open, and she sprung back to life.

"What happened?" she asked.

"You passed out."

"Oh, my goodness. I'm so embarrassed. I'm sorry."

"You have no reason to apologize. You have every right to feel the way you do. You're going through right now."

She tried propping herself up to a sitting position, but her body resisted.

"You might want to wait a few minutes before you try

moving," Raine said. "Can I get you something? Water or something to eat? Are you hungry?"

She shook her head. "I don't think I could handle food right now."

Raine sat beside her. "I'm just as confused as you are about everything."

Anne studied Raine's face and then said, "Did you know your sister was sleeping with my husband?"

"I didn't."

"What about Seth?"

"He says he didn't know, and I believe him. He was shocked when he read your husband's note. He seems to think it's all true, but I'm not so sure."

Anne glanced at the front door. "I wonder why he isn't home yet."

"I think he needs some alone time."

"Did the police show you the note Jonas left?"

"I saw a photo of it. They asked me to confirm it was his handwriting, and I couldn't."

"Why not?"

"The words were slanted, which is similar to the way he wrote, but also different. It's hard to explain." She pushed herself into a sitting position, and this time, she managed to keep herself upright. "I may not be able to stomach food, but I think I'll take you up on that glass of water."

Raine grabbed a bottle of water from the pantry and brought it to her.

"Thanks," she said. "It's weird to me, you know? Of all the women he could have cheated on me with, I'm shocked he would choose Juliette."

"Why?"

She twisted the cap on the water bottle and took a sip. "He had a type. She's not it."

"To be honest, he didn't seem like her *type,* either."

"When we had dinner the other night, Jonas acted like his usual self. It didn't seem like anything was on his mind. He was flirting with me and—"

She stopped midsentence.

"What were you going to say?" Raine asked.

"I just remembered something. Jonas received a phone call right as we were sitting down for dinner. It's uncommon for him to take calls if we're eating, but he took it. He was private about it, though."

"In what way?"

"He went into another room and closed the door."

"Do you know who called him?"

"I don't. He just said it was an important work thing he hadn't finished."

"What time was the call?"

"Let's see. Around six thirty."

"How long did it last?"

"A few minutes."

"I hear they haven't been able to locate your husband's phone."

"He had two. One work phone, one personal. The police officers I spoke to this evening said the same thing. Jonas always kept his phones in his pocket. I was surprised they weren't on his person when he died."

Yet another reason Raine favored foul play over suicide.

"After the phone call, did Jonas act any different?" Raine asked. "Or did he say anything about it?"

Anne gave the question some thought. "His demeanor was different, yes, and he wasn't as playful as he'd been before the call. We had dinner, and after, we said our goodbyes, and I headed to my father's house."

"When you spoke to Jonas this morning, what details did he give about the vacation he wanted to take with you?"

Anne chugged some of the water down and then set the bottle on the coffee table. "He wanted the location of the trip to be a surprise, so I wasn't given any details. He was going to pick me up at my father's place, and we'd fly out from there."

"Did you two travel a lot?"

She shook her head. "We haven't gone on a vacation together in over a year. Thinking back on it now, the entire call was odd. He didn't want me to come home first. He wanted to pack my things for me. He's never done anything like that before."

"There's something I should tell you," Raine said. "I've been working with Detective Ford on the investigation, and when he brought me back to the house earlier, there was a note in the mailbox. It was from Jonas."

"Now, that is a surprise. What did it say?"

Raine relayed the note's contents to Anne, who pressed a hand to her lips. "I don't know what to say. It doesn't sound like something he'd do."

"I don't have the note, but Ford let me take a picture of it." Raine pulled the photo up on her phone, then turned the screen toward Anne. "Do you know if this is his handwriting?"

Anne leaned in for a closer look and then nodded. "It's his. I'm positive."

35

F *ord*

The Prosperity Investments building looked like every other financial firm Ford had ever stepped into with its neutral walls, polished floors, and the faint hum of money being made. But a few details set it apart. Aside from the owner, no one appeared to have an office. The entire floor was a single, open rectangle, with desks aligned in precise rows with no partitions or cubicle walls. The layout allowed a clear view from one end of the room to the other, a design that seemed to favor surveillance over privacy.

Ford counted a couple dozen employees, all men. Every one of them was in similar suits, like they'd all showed up to audition for the same role. And they all looked similar in age, mid-thirties Ford guessed.

Today Ford was joined by Detective Whitaker. He'd left

Raine's side for a short time, but she was in capable hands, with two officers outside, and a third in the house.

Whitaker approached one of the employees, and once he stated their reasons for being there, they were ushered into an office and told their boss was in a meeting, and he'd join them as soon as he became available.

A few minutes later, a tall, muscular man in a blue suit entered the room, smiling as he stuck out his hand. "Thank you both for waiting. I'm Maxwell Duran, but you can call me Max. I assume you're both here about Jonas."

Whitaker nodded. "We're looking to corroborate a few facts surrounding his death."

Max took a seat, crossing one leg over the other. "Of course. Ask me anything," but before a question could be posed, he grabbed a crystal decanter off a metal cart and poured himself a drink.

Holding the glass in the air, he turned to Ford and Whitaker. "Would anyone care to join me? I assume you're both on the clock, but I won't tell. And I can guarantee one thing—this whiskey is better than any you've ever tried before."

"One of your employees is dead," Ford said. "If you could sit down and take this meeting seriously, we'd appreciate it."

Max gave Ford a look like he wasn't used to be spoken to in such a manner, then he nodded and took a seat.

"I apologize if pouring myself a drink came across as rude," he said. "It wasn't my intention. It's been a long day, and there are many heavy hearts around the office. I've spent most of it consoling my staff, and now I'm just trying to unwind. I'm sure, in your line of work, the two of you can appreciate that."

Whitaker leaned forward, resting his elbows on his knees. "Were you aware of the relationship between Jonas Parr and his neighbor, Juliette Granger?"

"What makes you think he had a relationship with his neighbor?"

Whitaker took out his cell phone, flipped through a few photos, and then handed the phone to Max, showing him the alleged suicide note Jonas had left behind.

Max mumbled through the words in the note, and then said, "I don't know what to say. I never met anyone other than his wife. He kept his private life private."

"What about a woman named Sadie Tucker?" Ford asked. "Did he ever mention her?"

Max shook his head. "I'm sorry, no. Who is she?"

Ford ignored the question. "Did you know Jonas owned a condo downtown?"

"Absolutely. He came to me when he was considering the purchase, and he asked for my opinion on whether it was a good deal. It was a tremendous one, well below market value. I advised him to go for it, and he did."

Ford found Max's choice of words peculiar. "Absolutely" and "tremendous," two unnecessary superlatives, stood out like red flags. They were the kind of embellishments people used when they wanted to sound convincing, not truthful. If Max had known about the condo, why dress his words up in such a way?

"I find it interesting he told you about the condo when you just said he kept his private life private," Ford said.

"They're two different things, now aren't they? Asking for advice about a condo is a lot different than discussing his personal relationships."

"It seems to us that he purchased the place with the intention of letting Sadie live there."

Max crossed one leg over the other. "I couldn't say. Jonas never offered an explanation about why he was interested in getting a second place, and I never asked for one. For all I knew, he planned to use it as an investment."

"How would you describe the relationship you had with Jonas?"

"It was the typical boss, employee relationship. It centered around work. He was a good man and a hard worker. His death is a great loss to the company and to everyone who works here."

Ford's attention shifted to a framed photo on Max's desk of a man in a crisp military uniform, standing tall with the kind of posture that didn't fade with age. The resemblance was unmistakable. It was Max, years younger, his face leaner. Ford studied it a moment longer, wondering what kind of man Max had been back then, and how much of that man he was now.

Max seemed to notice Ford's interest, and he picked up the frame, smiling as he gazed upon it. "Miss those days, you know? Seems like a world away now. You ever enlist?"

Ford shook his head. "What was your position?"

"Special Operations Commander."

"How long did you serve?"

"Long enough. After I retired, I realized sitting around all day didn't suit me. Guess you could say I'm a workaholic, which is easy given I don't have much of a personal life. No time for it."

"How long did Jonas work for you?"

"Five years."

"I'd like to see his workstation."

"It isn't possible."

"Why not?"

"Jonas didn't have an office. He spent most of his time out in the field, meeting with our biggest clients. Keeping them happy was his specialty." He took a long swallow from his glass, then set it down on a folder in front of him. "What I don't understand is why you're still questioning people. If Jonas left a suicide note confessing to killing his neighbor, it sounds to me like you already found your killer."

"There's still a lot that we still don't know yet," Whitaker said. "Too many loose ends. We're just making sure we have the answers we need before we close the case."

"I understand, and I'd like to help in any way I can."

Whitaker turned toward Ford. "I've asked all my questions. Do you have anything else you'd like to say before we leave?"

Ford considered how far to push and decided today he was in a pushing kind of mood. "What would you say if I told you Juliette Granger's daughter might still be alive, and that we believe she was in Sadie's condo?"

Whitaker shot Ford an irritated look, but Ford didn't flinch.

He was done tiptoeing around people who couldn't, or wouldn't, speak the truth. Too many of their interviews had felt like performances, half-truths dressed up as honesty.

Besides, the note Jonas left hadn't even been made public yet, and Whitaker hadn't hesitated before he showed it to Max.

"I can see how everyone is holding out hope that the little girl is still alive, but why would Jonas admit to burying her if he hadn't?" Max asked.

The longer Ford sat there, the more certain he became that something about Max didn't sit right. His answers were too polished, his timing too careful. Ford couldn't prove it yet, but Max knew more than he was letting on. Ford was sure of it.

He decided not to respond to Max's question, and he stood, saying, "Thanks for your time. If we have any further questions, we'll be in touch."

As he turned toward the door, he caught a glimpse of Max's reflection in the office window and the faint smirk on his face, like a man who knew something Ford didn't.

36

Whitaker scratched the back of his head, squinting against the afternoon sun. "Why in the world did you tell Max Duran privileged information about Sadie Tucker?"

Ford shut his truck door and leaned against it, arms folded. "You showed him the suicide note. I didn't think what I mentioned was a big deal in comparison. And besides, I didn't tell him anything crucial."

Whitaker shook his head, unconvinced. "Still. You've got to be more careful. Guys like that don't miss much."

"Yeah, I know," Ford said. "You notice anything off about him?"

Whitaker frowned. "Off? Like what?"

"The way he talked, for starters. Every word sounded rehearsed, like he'd practiced what he was going to say in front of a mirror."

"He seemed fine to me. A little theatrical, maybe, but not unusual."

"He lied to us," Ford said.

Whitaker turned his head, studying him. "And what makes you so sure of that?"

"Gut feeling," Ford replied.

"All right, then. What do you think he's lying about?"

Ford glanced at the reflection of the Prosperity Investments building in the car's windshield. "I'm not so sure he knew about the condo Jonas bought. I suspect he'd heard about it, but maybe from someone other than Jonas."

"Why lie about something so trivial?"

"I'm not sure yet. All I know is it's gnawing at me. And if he's hiding something, I'm going to find out what."

A breeze stirred, carrying the faint hum of traffic from the nearby road. Whitaker said nothing, and for a long moment, neither did Ford. Then Ford glanced up toward Max's window and saw the blinds shift, as if someone inside was watching them. And in that moment, something told him he'd be seeing more of Max before the case was over.

37

R*aine*

Seth still wasn't home, and Raine had done everything in her power to reach him. She'd texted, and she'd called. Still nothing. She was halfway through sending another text when a call came through.

"I'm on my way back over to you," Ford said. "You holding up okay?"

"I was just going to call you. I'm with Jonas's wife, Anne. She said he received a phone call last night at dinner, and he seemed bothered by it."

"What time?" Ford asked.

Raine told him.

"Hang on, let me pull over."

She held on.

Then she heard what sounded like the shuffling of paper.

Seconds later, he returned to the line.

"We may not have his phone, but the records were sent over today. There were no incoming or outgoing calls made around that time. What was the call about?"

"She doesn't know. He excused himself and took it in his office. Oh, and she also told me Jonas had two phones, a work phone and a personal one."

"Huh, has Seth shown up yet?"

"He hasn't."

"Any idea where he's at?"

"Not a clue."

He went quiet for so long she thought the call had dropped. Then his voice came back, low and hesitant. "A woman is missing. Her name is Sadie Tucker."

"Is Sadie related to the case somehow?"

"When the police ran a search on the condo she's living in, they discovered she doesn't own it, Jonas does—or *did*."

"We still aren't sure whether she was renting the place from him, or if they were involved in some way."

"How long has she been missing?"

"We don't know."

"How do you know she's missing, then?"

"Sadie's next-door neighbor called the police late last night. She was in bed and said she could hear what sounded like a little girl crying on the other side of the wall."

"Does Sadie have children?"

"She doesn't," he said. "The neighbor said she couldn't take the crying anymore, so she and her husband went over and knocked on the door. Sadie answered looking worn out. She had dark circles under her eyes and looked like she hadn't gotten much sleep. When the neighbor asked about the girl, Sadie wouldn't talk about her. All she said was the kid wouldn't be there long."

"The neighbor didn't happen to see the child, did she?"

"While they were talking, a little girl wandered into the hallway. Sadie snapped at her, telling her to get back to bed. The neighbor went home, but a couple hours later, she turned on the TV and saw the missing-person alert. The picture that came up on the screen reminded her of the child she'd seen."

Raine's hands shook so much she struggled to keep hold of the phone.

Could it be true?

Could her niece still be alive?

"Have the police been to the house?" Raine asked.

"They have, but no one came to the door. They went back again this morning with a search warrant. When they went inside, there was no sign of Sadie Tucker, but her car is still parked in the garage."

"So, what happens now?"

"They've collected some hair samples and lifted a few prints from the home. The forensic team is running tests as we speak."

"How sure is the neighbor that the girl she saw was Nora?"

"Both the woman and her husband believe the girl they saw is Nora. I need you and Anne, if she's listening, to keep what I've just told you to yourselves for now, okay? We haven't released any of this information to the public."

"Sure, no problem."

"While I have you, I'm going to text you a photo of a child's toy. Take a look and tell me if you recognize it."

Raine pulled the phone away from her ear and stared at the screen, waiting. A few seconds later, an attachment appeared. She tapped it open, and the moment the image filled the screen, she gasped.

The photo was of a unicorn.

A stuffed pink unicorn.

Raine put the call on speaker. "I recognize the stuffed animal. It's Nora's."

"Are you sure?"

"I bought it for her. Where did you find it?"

"Under the bed in Sadie's spare bedroom."

"If this is true—"

"It calls everything in the note Jonas left into question."

"Where is the stuffed animal now?" Raine asked.

"Zipped in a bag in an evidence locker, waiting on forensic testing," he said. "Why?"

"Tell someone to squeeze the alicorn."

"The ... what now?"

"The horn on the unicorn's head. It's called an alicorn. They should hear a recording of my voice, saying, 'Happy birthday, sweetheart. Auntie Raine loves you.'"

"Can I put you on hold again for a minute?"

Raine agreed and the line went silent.

A few minutes passed, and Ford returned to the call. "You still there?"

"I am. What did you find out?"

"You're right. The unicorn ... it's Nora's."

38

Raine ended the call with Ford and turned toward Anne, filling her in on the conversation they'd just had.

"Did you know Jonas owned a condo?" Raine asked.

The shock on her face gave Raine her answer.

"There has to be a mistake," Anne said. "Our house is the only one we own. If there were another, I'd know about it."

Anne reminded Raine of Seth in some ways. Juliette and Jonas didn't seem like the right fit for each other, but Anne and Seth, she could see it.

"Ford just told me Jonas owned a condo in the city," Raine said. "He seems certain about it. A woman named Sadie has been living there."

Anne fiddled with her wedding ring, twisting it around her finger like she was frustrated. "Does Seth have any wine around here? I don't care how off my stomach today. I need it."

Raine searched the kitchen cabinets until she came across a bottle of merlot and two glasses. She pulled the cork free and filled each glass.

"Thank you," Anne said as Raine handed her a glass. "Now,

about Jonas and this Sadie woman, maybe some background will help. I met Jonas in high school, and through all the years we were together, I never doubted that he loved me. What I did doubt was his faithfulness. There were other women, though I never knew how many."

"How long have you suspected him of being unfaithful?"

"Depends on what you mean by unfaithful," she said. "It started when we were still teenagers. Jonas never did understand boundaries. Since we married, I've known about at least three women. If Sadie was one of them, that makes four. And your sister, five."

"Did he ever suspect you knew about his affairs?"

Anne shook her head. "He's always treated me like some clueless airhead, but I'm not. When I found out about the first woman, I was ready to confront him. I remember thinking that no matter what he said—whether he admitted it, promised to stop, or said nothing at all—it wouldn't change anything. I was hurt, but I knew I wouldn't leave him."

"Why not?"

Anne took a sip of wine. "I loved him. I bet you think I was a fool for staying when most women would have walked away."

Raine knew she could never stay with a man who wasn't loyal, yet she understood how loving someone as much as Anne loved Jonas could make walking away impossible. "It's not my place to judge you."

"You are judging me, though. I can tell. Have you ever been cheated on?"

"I haven't."

"Then you don't know what you'd do."

"I suppose I can see your point."

Anne stared past Raine, focusing on a magnetic photo of Seth and Juliette on the fridge. "Have you ever loved a man so much the thought of being without that person made your insides hurt? I felt that way about Jonas."

Raine had never allowed herself to love anyone in such a way, always choosing to guard her heart. But sitting across from Anne, she began to wonder if she'd been wrong. Maybe in protecting herself from pain, she'd also shut out the kind of love that made life worth living.

"Did you say anything to the police about his affairs?" Raine asked.

"I haven't yet, and I know I should have. I'm embarrassed, I guess, and I wanted to believe admitting it wouldn't make a difference because he's dead. Now that this woman has gone missing, I'll tell them everything, as much as I know."

Anne tipped her head back, downing the last of the wine in her glass. Then she hopped off the counter and poured herself another.

"Jonas went for women who were a little rough around the edges and wild—my opposite. The women he chased and the life we shared felt like two halves of him. There was the reckless side that drove him and the softer side that needed someone calm to steady it."

Admitting her husband's affairs had taken a toll on her. Even with the wine easing her nerves, Raine could see her struggling to hold herself together.

"It's hard when the unexpected happens, isn't it?" Raine asked. "I question everything now. My sister's death. Jonas's death. What happened to Nora. I wish I knew where to find the answers."

"I'm with you there."

They sat in silence for a moment, and then Raine said, "If you don't mind, I'd like to know a little more about the job Jonas had."

"He managed hedge funds for Prosperity Investments."

Hedge funds, a sticky business, which could also prove dangerous if Jonas angered the wrong kind of people. Money was a drug. It had the ability to make people crazy—even crazier when they lost it.

"How long did he work there?" Raine asked.

"Five years. He started after he retired from the military."

Raine didn't know why, but his military service surprised her. "What was his job in the military?"

"He was a sniper." Anne turned away, frowning. "I'll admit, I wasn't honest with you just now. Jonas didn't retire from the military. He was discharged several years ago for bad conduct."

"What happened?"

"He was driving one of the tanks one night. It was dark. A soldier crossed in front of it. Jonas didn't see him until it was too late. He hit the solider, and the solider died."

"He was discharged for accidentally killing someone?"

"Not just killing him. The soldier's death could have been prevented. At the time, Jonas had been drinking."

"I see."

"Thing is, he hated the guy, the one he killed. I don't think everyone else knew that, but I did. He complained about him all the time."

"Are you saying you question whether the man's death was an accident?"

Anne nodded. "Jonas swore it was an accident, but it's never sat well with me. And now, after what's happened with Juliette and Nora, I feel my suspicions were right."

"What happened after he was discharged?"

"He wanted to live in a place where he could leave it all behind, so we moved here."

To Vegas?

To Raine, leaving it all behind and starting fresh would take a person to a small town. Somewhere cozy and inviting. Not to sin city.

"Did Jonas have any background in investments before you moved here?" Raine asked.

"None."

"And yet he went from being a sniper to an investment banker?"

"I know. I thought the same thing at first. I never pictured him shuffling papers around at some desk job. He isn't the type. He was good at it, though. His boss, Max Duran, saw his potential right away and moved him into a higher position."

Raine set her half-finished glass in the sink, her stomach too knotted up to take another sip. "What made Jonas apply for the job in the first place?"

"He didn't apply. He got a phone call from someone who worked at the investment company. They knew he was no longer in the military and that he'd moved to Las Vegas, looking for a job."

"So, the job just fell into his lap?"

"Yeah, I guess. He interviewed, and they liked him. I'm not surprised. He was always gifted at charming people. I guess he got lucky."

He got lucky all right.

He'd married a woman who never questioned the stories he told, no matter how many holes they had in them. But every lie runs out of road eventually, and for Jonas, his had met its end.

39

A*nne*

Anne was packing a few clothes into a suitcase when the doorbell rang. Thinking she was running behind, she checked the time, but her friend wasn't due to arrive for another twenty minutes.

She paused at the door, glancing out the window to see who was standing on the other side—Max.

Anne had always liked Max, and even though she'd only seen him a few times over the years, he'd always gone out of his way to make her feel welcome. Thinking back on those times now, she realized she'd looked forward to those moments far more than she wanted to admit.

She opened the door to a bouquet of roses, their scent faint but comforting. Max stood behind them, his eyes clouded with sympathy.

"I wanted to bring you these, and I also wanted to see how you're holding up," he said. "I hope it's not a bad time."

"It's fine. I appreciate you taking the time to stop by."

She stepped aside to let him in, and together they walked to the kitchen. Anne opened a cabinet, retrieved a vase, and carried it to the sink. As the water ran, she guided each stem into place, adjusting them until the bouquet took shape.

"I appreciate the flowers," she said.

"The flowers are just the beginning. I'd like to do more. Tell me what you need, how I can help."

She glanced over at him and bit down on her lip, trying to stop the tears. They came anyway.

"I'm sorry," she said.

"I'm the one who should be sorry. I came here hoping to offer some comfort, but it seems all I've done is make things harder for you."

"Oh, no. I'm glad you're here. It's good to see you. It's been a while."

He approached, pulling her into an embrace, the kind that came from genuine concern rather than affection. It was steady and reassuring, and she let herself rest in it for a moment before stepping back.

"I'm so sorry about Jonas," he said. "We all are."

"I still can't believe what's happened."

"It was a shock to us all."

She brushed the tears from her cheeks, her voice unsteady.

"I ... I ... don't even know what's real anymore. Jonas had a condo I knew nothing about, and a woman was living there. She's missing now. And in the note Jonas left, he said he'd buried Nora, but they found something belonging to her in that condo. The detectives think she might still be alive." She drew in a shaky breath. "It's too much to take in."

She'd spoken without thinking, forgetting Raine's warning to keep that information quiet until the police released the details to the public. But Max wasn't just anyone. He was a friend.

"I spoke to the police earlier today," Max said. "They made no mention about a discovery at the condo. What did they find?"

"A stuffed animal."

"How can they be sure it's Nora's?"

She considered telling him about the birthday message, then decided against it.

"I don't know," she said.

He raised a brow, eyeing her like he questioned whether she was telling the truth. "If it is the child's stuffed animal, it changes things, doesn't it? Maybe Jonas wasn't telling the truth after all. Maybe the little one is still out there somewhere."

"I hope so."

There was a knock at the door.

"Are you expecting someone?" Max asked.

She nodded. "I have a friend staying with me for a few days. The police have been coming in and out, and I don't want to be here alone."

"I understand, and I won't keep you."

Anne walked him to the door, introducing him to her friend when she opened it. He stepped onto the porch, and she said, "Thank you again for the flowers."

"It's the least I can do," he said. "I'd like to give you a call tomorrow to check in if that's all right?"

"Of course."

"Oh, I almost forgot." Reaching into his pocket, he pulled out a thick envelope and handed it to her. "This is for you. A little something to help with the funeral arrangements."

"Thank you, but I can't accept it."

He slipped the envelope into her hand, resting his palm over hers. "The time we've spent together, even if it wasn't much, meant a lot to me. And Jonas ... well, he was like a brother. It gives me peace to take care of you during this tough time."

He pulled his hand away, and she told herself the warmth he left behind was comfort. Still, as she stared at the envelope of cash, a faint chill ran through her, one she couldn't explain.

40

S *eth*

At two o'clock in the morning, Seth staggered out of the third bar he'd drifted into over the past twenty-four hours. The night air hit him like a slap—cool, sharp, and sobering—but not enough to clear the haze clouding his head.

Neon lights bled into puddles along the sidewalk as he made his way down the street, first one way, then the other, trying to remember where he'd parked his truck.

Five minutes passed, then ten, and there was still no sign of his vehicle. He frowned, spinning in place, but all he saw was an empty stretch of road and the faint hum of a streetlight flickering overhead.

His stomach growled, the sound breaking the quiet. He couldn't remember the last time he'd eaten. Then it came to him. It was the pot roast Juliette made the night she left, the night his life changed forever. He could still picture her at the stove, ladling gravy over the meat, pretending everything was fine. He'd sat across from her, having no idea it was the last meal they'd ever share together.

His legs felt like bricks, each step heavier than the last, and he bent down, sitting on the curb. For a moment, he just sat there, staring at the pavement, trying to piece the night together. Everything about the day was a fog, one long, staggering blur of whiskey and regret. And the more he tried to remember, the further the memory slipped from his reach.

He fumbled for his phone and squinted, scrolling through his contacts until he spotted a name beginning with R, and he tapped on it.

Nothing.

With a muttered curse, he tried again. This time it rang for what seemed like forever, but the, someone answered.

"Seth?" Raine said. "Where are you?"

"Hey, Raine."

"What time is it?"

"Late, or early, depending on how you look at it."

"I've been trying to reach you all day. Are you all right?"

"Can you come get me?" he asked.

"Where are you?"

"I'm at a bar. I mean I *was* at a bar. I was going to sleep in my truck for a while until I sobered up. Problem is, I can't find it."

"Where are you?"

He stood and looked for the sign over the bar he'd walked out of minutes before, but he didn't see it. "Umm, let me think. It's the one with the red blinking lights around the sign, and it has a woman on it. She kind of looks like a cartoon, and she's sitting inside a martini glass."

"Can you remember the name of the place?"

Legs shaky and weak, he leaned against a pole, glancing down the street. "I need to find the sign. I'll call you back."

"No, Seth. Wait. Don't hang up. There's something I need to tell—"

"It's fine. I'll call you back."

He ended the call and began walking. A few minutes later, a car pulled up beside him. A man around his age lowered the window and smiled, saying, "Hey there. How's it going?"

Seth glanced around, assuming the man was talking to someone else, then realized he was talking to him.

"Hey, do you know the name of the bar on this street, the one with the red lights around the sign?" Seth asked.

"Sure do. It's The Crimson Ale."

"Oh, yeah. And which direction is it?"

The man pointed.

"I don't know how I got so turned around, but I appreciate your help."

He started walking again, his footsteps uneven on the cracked pavement. After a few seconds, he noticed the car beside him was moving too, matching his pace.

"You need a ride, right?" the man asked.

Seth shook his head. "I have someone coming for me. Well, she will be. I was just talking to her, but I couldn't remember the name of the bar. I need to call her back."

"Are you Seth?"

Seth stopped, turning toward the man. "Do we know each other?"

"I was sent to pick you up," the man said. "I'm with Drivio."

"I didn't call you. I mean, I don't think I did."

"Your friend scheduled the ride."

Seth could have sworn Raine said she was coming to pick him up. But maybe he was wrong. Maybe she'd sent someone else instead. He hadn't given her the name of the bar he was at, though. Had he?

"Seems like you've had a lot to drink tonight," the man said.

Seth nodded. "Been at it eight hours at least. And just so you know, I don't do this ... drink, I mean. But today ... well, today is different. Hey, how do I know you were sent to pick me up?"

"You live on 155 Nightshade Street, right?"

"Yeah."

The man got out of the car, walked around it, and opened the passenger door. "Then you're the one I'm supposed to pick up. Go on, get in."

Seth looked at the passenger seat, then at the man. "Don't you want me to sit in back?"

"Naw, up front's fine."

Maybe Raine *had* sent him. The guy knew his name and his address, and a car service would have made it there a lot faster than she would have.

Seth shrugged, dipped inside the car, and sat down.

The man walked back around to the driver's side, buckled himself in, and told Seth to do the same. Then he pulled out onto the street.

"I like this seat," Seth said. "It's comfortable."

"It has a massage feature, if you're interested."

"Are you serious?"

The man nodded and pressed a button on a touchscreen monitor in the center of the dashboard.

"Wow, that's amazing," Seth said.

The man nodded. "It's one of the reasons I bought this car."

Seth leaned back and put the window down part way. "Sorry, I need air. I'm feeling a little nauseous, and I don't want to get sick in your car."

"No problem. I hope this doesn't offend you, but I think I saw you on the news earlier this evening."

Seth's eyes widened, but he said nothing.

"They showed a picture of your family," the man said.

"What picture?"

"It looked like a family photo."

"I'm not surprised. A few reporters have stopped by the house, trying to get me to talk to them about ... You know what? It doesn't matter. It's inconsiderate, you know? I'm grieving. They don't care about me, or my wife, or our daughter. All they're after is a story."

"I heard what happened. I'm sorry."

"I didn't know they had my picture. Maybe my sister-in-law gave it to them. What else did they say?"

The man tapped a thumb to the steering wheel. "Let's see. I don't recall everything, but I do remember them saying that right after your wife's accident, your next-door neighbor committed suicide."

"He'd been having an affair with my wife. My best friend and my wife. Can you believe it? Who does that?"

"Oh, man. How awful. I can't imagine what you're going through."

Seth ran a hand through his hair, his voice unsteady. "Yeah. The four of us used to hang out sometimes. And you know what's strange? My wife never acted like she had feelings for him. Not once. Every time we went out, he couldn't keep his hands off his wife, and my wife used to say they were the perfect couple. I thought so too."

"Had she ever cheated on you before?"

"Maybe. I'm not sure."

"What do you mean?"

Fragments of past memories raced through Seth's mind, but he was intoxicated. Perhaps too intoxicated to remember. "My wife ... she, ahh, she used to talk in her sleep. One night, she sat straight up in bed and started mumbling a name over and over

—Maxwell."

"Maxwell? No last name?"

"Nope, and you know, it could have all been a dream. And if it wasn't, Maxwell could be a first or a last name. Who knows?"

"Did she say anything else?"

Seth reached his hand out of the car window, brushing it against the night air. "She did. She said, 'Maxwell, I love you.'"

"Huh. Strange."

"Not as strange as my neighbor admitting they'd been having an affair."

"Do you know anyone with a first or last name of Maxwell?"

"I don't." The streets swayed around Seth, their colors dull and blurred, melting together like wet paint being washed out by rain. "Hey, where are we?"

"We're about ten minutes from your house."

"Sorry for talking your ear off."

"You've been through a rough couple of days. The least I can do is let you get it out of your system."

Seth laughed. "I have a sister-in-law for that."

"What's *she* like?"

"Stubborn, but smart. Smartest person I know. She isn't convinced my neighbor's responsible for what happened, not even after reading the suicide note he left behind admitting he did it. There's a cop she's working with, and he's not sure he believes what was in the note, either.

"I'm surprised to hear it. The news made it sound like the police were wrapping everything up."

"Sorry, the alcohol's gone to my head. They guy she's been talking to—he's not a cop. He's a detective. He was on the scene when they found my wife. He's working with the local police."

The man reached a hand into the side panel of his door, pulled out a bottle of water, and offered it to Seth. "Meant to hand this to you earlier. After the day you've had, you need to hydrate."

Seth shook his head. "No, thanks. My stomach is still a bit queasy."

The man handed him the water anyway. "You should still drink it. It has electrolytes. It will help you feel better."

Seth wrenched the cap off the bottle and took a few sips, hoping the man was right. "Hey, thanks."

"No problem."

"By the way, what's your name?"

The man looked over, a crooked smile on his face as he said, "It's Adam."

41

R *aine*

Raine waited for a return call from Seth, a call that never came, and there was no point going out looking for him unless she knew his location. There were thousands of bars in Las Vegas. It was impossible to know where to look. All she had to go on was the comment he'd made about red lights around a sign and a woman inside a martini glass. In a city known for its dazzling lights, he could have been talking about any number of places.

Raine got out of bed and walked to the living room, trying to decide whether to wake up Ford, who was sleeping on the couch. But when she passed by, she noticed he was awake.

He looked up at her, a look of concern on his face. "Every-thing okay?"

"I'm not sure. I got a call from Seth about ten minutes ago. He'd just left a bar, and he sounded drunk. He said he couldn't find his truck, and he wanted me to come and pick him up. But he didn't remember the name of the bar he was at. He was going to figure it out and call me back, and he hasn't yet."

"Did he give you any useful information about where he was at?"

"He said sign on the bar had red blinking lights, and a woman sitting inside a martini glass."

"Hang on a second. Let me make a call."

Ford sat up and reached for his cell phone. He made a call, then turned toward Raine and said, "One of the guys at the department thinks the bar is The Crimson Ale. Shall we head over, see if we can find him?"

Raine nodded. "Let me grab a sweater."

A few minutes later, she returned to the living room, sweater in hand. "I think someone's been through my things. A few of the shirts I had in one of Nora's drawers aren't folded anymore, and I was sure I put my car keys in my purse, but when I went to grab it, I found them sitting beside the bag, not in it."

"You think someone's been here?"

"I think it's possible. I was here most of the day, except for the short time we went to the jewelry store."

"We've had cops out front since this morning. If someone got in, they managed to come and go without being seen, which is a problem. I'll talk to the officers out front on our way out and have them clear the house while we're gone."

Raine nodded and wrapped her sweater around her, and they headed for Ford's truck. After a quick chat with the officers, they made their way to the bar, driving in silence for a time.

Then Ford said, "The day we met, you said you weren't married. You also said you don't date. Why not?"

"You're asking me that *now*?"

"It's a twenty-minute drive. I thought it would be nice to

talk about something light for a change. If I was out of line by asking the question, I apologize."

"It's fine. Are you married?"

"Widowed."

"I'm sorry."

"Don't be. She's been gone for a while now. I've made my peace with it."

"Have you dated at all since she passed?"

"A bit. Nothing serious."

Raine stared out the window, thinking about how much personal information she was willing to give. "I'm not opposed to having a relationship. I'm just cautious. There was a time in my life when I put serious effort into trying to find someone, and then that time passed."

"Can I ask what happened?"

"For years I was always falling for the wrong guy. And even though it was a pattern I repeated, I didn't recognize it for the longest time. The guys I dated looked different, but their personalities were similar."

"May I ask what kind of personality that might be?"

"Machiavellian."

"Ahh, self-serving and manipulative, always putting themselves first."

Raine nodded. "I reached a point where I knew I had to either learn how to recognize it when I started seeing someone new or stop dating altogether. I started therapy, and it changed everything. Now, I can spot that type of guy from across the room."

"Is there a reason you haven't started dating again?"

"I wanted to take my time, to start dating again when it felt right. I kept telling myself I was fine on my own, but maybe that was just a way to avoid admitting how lonely it gets sometimes."

"I suppose I've been doing the same thing."

Raine rested an elbow on the window ledge. "Would you mind if we talked about something else?"

"Sure, why don't you pick the topic this time?"

"When I spoke to Anne yesterday, she told me Jonas used to be a sniper in the military. He was dishonorably discharged for killing a fellow soldier. Jonas claimed it was an accident, but Anne suspected he may have killed the guy on purpose. She said he hated him."

"Interesting. When I talked to Max earlier today, the man Jonas worked for, he had a photo on his desk of him dressed in a miliary uniform. I asked him about it. He said he used to be a Special Operations Commander. I'm pretty sure the Special Ops Commander is over Special Forces."

To Raine, it seemed like too big of a coincidence not to mean something.

"Anne said Jonas didn't have any background in investments when he was hired. From the way she told it, the job seemed to come out of nowhere."

They turned onto a side street and eased the truck to a stop in front of the bar. The place was dark, its windows empty, the street around it silent and still.

Ford pointed at the sign. "The sign looks like what Seth described to you, doesn't it?"

"It does."

"While we're looking for him, we should also try to find his truck. If it's here, I'm guessing it's close by."

"Let's find out."

They found Seth's truck parked less than a block from the bar, and the door was unlocked when they tried it. Raine leaned in, catching the faint scent of whiskey and stale cologne. The driver's seat was pushed back, a jacket crumpled across it. She'd hoped to find Seth there, sleeping off the night's drinks. But he wasn't there.

For the next hour, they circled the nearby streets, covering the same few blocks multiple times. With each pass, Raine's unease grew stronger, a steady, gnawing sense that something had gone wrong.

It seemed Seth hadn't just wandered off.

He'd disappeared.

42

S *eth*

Seth blinked hard, the world around him slowly coming into focus. He was on a leather couch, the cushions creased and cool beneath his palms. The room he was in was dim, almost claustrophobic, lit only by a single lamp on a small round table beside him.

He pushed himself to an upright position, the movement sending a wave of dizziness through him. His hand went to the side of his head, where a dull ache throbbed just above his temple. When his fingers brushed the spot, he flinched. It felt tender, but there didn't seem to be any swelling. The pain wasn't skin-deep. It pulsed from somewhere inside, a deep, rhythmic pounding that made it hard to think straight.

A migraine, maybe.

Or something worse.

He tried to retrace his steps, to remember how he'd gotten

here, but his thoughts slipped away before he could catch them. The room was unfamiliar—no windows, no clock, just the low hum of silence pressing in on him.

The last thing he remembered was climbing into the front seat of a man's car. The details were hazy, but he remembered asking the man for his name. He was sure it started with an A.

Alex?

No.

Aaron?

That wasn't it either.

He rubbed his temples, forcing his thoughts into focus.

Then, like a light flicking on, it came to him.

Adam.

Was that whose house he was in?

He stood, walked to the double doors at the far end of the room, and tried to open them, shocked to discover he was locked in.

He balled his hand into a fist and pounded on it. "Hello? Is anyone there? Can anyone hear me?"

"It's nice to meet you, Mr. Granger," a male voice said.

The voice came from inside the room. Seth turned, scanning his surroundings a second time. In a dark corner, sitting on a chair, was a man dressed in a suit.

"You're not Adam," Seth said.

"No, I am not."

"Who are you? And why am I here? There was this guy, Adam. He's a Drivio driver. He picked me up from the bar and said he was taking me home. I remember getting into the car, but I don't remember what happened after. Do you know him?"

"Adam works for me."

"Oh, he didn't tell me he had a second job."

"He doesn't."

Seth felt like the man was talking in circles, answering his questions but remaining vague at the same time. "I'd like to leave now."

"Why don't I introduce myself? I know who you are. It's only fair you know who I am too."

Seth shrugged. "I don't see why it matters."

"My name is Maxwell Duran, but everyone calls me Max. You're in my home."

Maxwell.

It couldn't be.

And yet he was sure his suspicion would prove to be right.

"Did you know my wife?" he asked.

"I did. She was a wonderful woman. I was disappointed things ended with her the way they did. Such a shame. I'd hoped we would have had more time together."

The way Max spoke about Juliette carried an undertone Seth couldn't ignore, one that suggested their relationship had been intimate. The realization turned his stomach. It had been hard enough coming to terms with the affair she'd had with Jonas, and now Max was hinting he'd had a place in her life too. Seth's pulse quickened, anger mixing with disbelief.

"I don't understand how I ended up here, what I'm doing here, or why," Seth said. "What do you want?"

"You were followed, Mr. Granger. Adam tailed you to the bar and then waited for you to leave. I have to say, I had no idea it was going to be such a long night. But it all worked out in the end. I asked him to bring you to my home, and here you are."

"Did you bring me here to tell me you slept with my wife? If so, get in line."

"The reason your head is pounding isn't from the alcohol. The water Adam gave you contained a mild drug, a sedative." Max extended his hand toward the leather couch. "Would you please sit back down?"

"No, I won't. Not until I know what's going on."

"It isn't like me to bring someone to my home, but at the moment, I have few options. And besides, you won't be staying long." Max crossed one leg over the other. "I want to give you an opportunity."

"An opportunity for what?"

"Is there anything you'd like to know about your wife and daughter?"

The only thing he wanted was the get the hell out of there, as far away from Max as possible. Maybe if he gave him what he wanted, maybe if he played whatever game he was playing, Max would allow him to leave.

"Well?" Max said. "Do you have questions, or don't you?"

"You say you knew my wife, but I don't know a thing about you."

"You have heard about me, though. I hear she called my name one night in her sleep."

Seth paused, then said, "Were you having a sexual relationship with my wife?"

"We were, yes."

"When did it start?"

"Four years ago. Would it surprise you to know that while you were out of town for work, she was often here, with me?"

The reality hit Seth like a punch to the gut, sharp and sudden, like it had knocked the air from his lungs.

"How did you two meet?" Seth asked.

"At Bellevue, after a tennis match. I was heading to my car when I saw her slipping her racket onto the seat of her car. She shut the door, turned toward me, and smiled. There was something in her eyes, boredom or loneliness, maybe both. She looked like someone desperate for something different, a better life perhaps. In that moment, I decided I'd be the one to give it to her."

"You're lying," Seth said. "She wasn't bored. She was happy. *We* were happy."

"If you believe that, I'm sorry to say you never knew your wife at all."

It was too much.

"I don't want to hear anymore," Seth said.

"I'm being honest with you. Isn't that what you want?"

"If Juliette wanted to be with you, why was she also sleeping with my next-door neighbor? And why did she stay married to me?"

"I have a second business in New York City. Most of the time, I coordinated my schedule so I would be here when you were out of town, but even then, our schedules didn't always work out. Juliette said she wouldn't give you up until I settled down in one place, a place where we could be together full time. I'll admit, it bothered me. I don't like to share. But I loved her, and I wanted the choice to be hers."

Seth had always thought of himself as a rational man, a man who was measured, patient, and in control. But right now, every trace of calm had been stripped away, replaced by a white-hot rage that burned through reason. He pictured his hands around Max's throat. And then, without thinking, he found himself lunging at him with all the fury he'd kept bottled inside.

Max remained calm, removing a pistol from the inside of his suit jacket.

Seth froze.

"Do yourself a favor and sit down, Mr. Granger."

Seth sat.

"I thought we were just talking," Seth said. "Why do you need a gun?"

"You're here because Juliette made a poor decision, and now everyone in her life is paying for it. Everyone, including Jonas."

"*Jonas?* You know him?"

"You've had a shock. I can't imagine what you're feeling right now. But this next part ... I guess what I'm trying to say is that whatever you're feeling now, it's about to get worse."

"I don't understand."

"Jonas worked for me."

"At the investment place?"

Max nodded.

All this time, Seth had thought Jonas was his friend. Now he started to wonder if he had been much more—Max's spy, someone he used to keep an eye on Juliette.

Juliette was dead.

Jonas was dead.

And Nora ...?

He replayed Ford's words from the day before in his mind, a theory that Jonas might not have taken his own life. If Jonas had been murdered, and if Max had played a part in it, had Jonas even had an affair with his wife?

"Was my wife's death an accident or did you mean to have her killed?" Seth asked. "It was you, wasn't it?"

"I ordered Juliette's death. Jonas was involved, but he wasn't the one who killed her."

It took every ounce of Seth's self-control to remain seated.

"And Jonas, did you have him murdered too?" Seth asked.

"I'm sure your mind is swirling with questions, but you need to ask yourself how important the truth is to you."

"I'm here, being held against my will. The least you can do is explain why you had someone kill my wife."

"All right, then. A couple of weeks ago, I hosted a party. After the event was over, I was in my office speaking to one of my employees. The conversation took a bad turn. We didn't see eye to eye, and I knew we never would. So, I shot him."

"You killed him, you mean."

"What matters is that Juliette walked in right after it happened. I thought she'd left for the night, but she'd forgotten her phone and had returned for it. I never heard her come in, and when she stepped into my office and saw what I'd done, she saw a side of me I never wanted her to see. After that, things between us changed. I tried to fix it, to make it better somehow. I never meant to kill her."

Seth swallowed hard. "Then why did you?"

"I warned Juliette not to tell anyone about what happened that night, and she promised to keep quiet. But as the days passed, she grew scared of me, and she began to unravel. And once something starts to come apart, it's almost impossible to stop it. You understand that, don't you?"

"No, I don't. All I hear is a man who was more concerned about his secret coming out than he was about a human life, or multiple human lives."

Max rested a hand over the gun in his lap. "I never planned on harming her, at first. Not until she decided to run. I tasked Jonas with dealing with it, and he went after her like he was told. But in the end, he couldn't go through with it, though I can't say I blame him. Thinking back, it was wrong of me to send him. If I was in the situation, if it was me pulling the trigger, I'm not sure I could have done it."

It didn't take much for Seth to see him for who he was, a man driven by self-preservation, no matter who stood in his way or how he claimed to feel about them.

Seth's throat tightened, and his voice broke as he forced the words out. "And Nora? What about her?"

"Ahh, yes. Nora. I was wondering when you would get to her. I apologize about not putting your mind at ease at the start of our conversation. Nora is alive, and she's doing just fine. Well, as fine as can be expected for now."

The news his daughter was, in fact, alive, left him elated

and gutted at the same time. What did they plan to do with her?

"Where is she?" Seth asked. "And why did the suicide note at Jonas's house say he buried her?"

"I needed everyone to believe Nora was dead. I wanted to tie up loose ends so the cops would close the investigation."

"I don't think they'll be backing away from it any time soon."

Max nodded. "I'm aware of the challenges I'm facing. No matter. All will be made right in the end."

The guy was insane.

A sociopath.

"If Nora's alive, where is she?" Seth asked.

"She's here, with me."

"*You* have her? Where? Why would you kill my wife and keep my daughter?"

"I believe you mean *my* daughter."

Seth tried to draw a breath but couldn't. He'd thought nothing Max said could be worse that what he'd already heard, but he was wrong. "*Your* daughter? She's not *your* daughter. You can't just take someone else's child and decide she's yours."

Max hesitated, his hand hovering over the gun. "You don't understand. I'm not claiming she's my daughter. She *is* my daughter. I had a DNA test done after she was born. You're a good man, Mr. Granger, a better man than I'll ever be. I'm sorry it had to end this way."

43

M *ax*

Max took one last puff of his cigar and leaned over, snubbing it out on a silver tray beside him. The past was over. It was time to restore the present and move on.

He glanced at the three men sitting across from him. "Tell me about Sadie Tucker."

"I got rid of her, just like you asked," Adam said. "Why?"

"A couple of detectives came to my office yesterday. They're looking for her. They seem to have proof Nora was in Sadie's condo."

"How is that possible?"

"Well, Adam, you tell me. Did you leave anything behind?"

"Anything like what?"

"A stuffed animal belonging to Nora."

Adam looked off to the side as if retracing the night in his mind. "I didn't see anything in the room she was in, and I took the bags I came in with when I left. Did I miss something?"

"You did. You forgot to look under the bed."

"Oh, my bad. I assumed she didn't have anything with her."

"Is there anything else I need to know, anything you haven't said? If there is, say it now."

Adam shook his head. "No one saw me enter the house, and no one saw me leave. It was a clean kill. Minimal blood. The kid was quiet. Those detectives have no idea what happened. They're just trying to rattle you."

Max crossed one leg over the other. "Perhaps."

Mark, another of Max's employees spoke up. "I was in the car while Adam took care of everything. He's right. No one saw a thing."

Victor added, "I have things to do. So, if you could hurry up and tell us why we're here, that would be great."

"You forget yourself, Victor," Max said.

Victor laughed. "I don't *forget* anything."

Max et the arrogant comment go for now. He'd drive the point home later when he had Victor alone.

"The reason why you're all here is because I have made a decision," Max said. "I'm halting all side business until everything blows over."

Victor grunted and slumped back in his chair. "For how long?"

"I don't know yet. I've considered leaving for a while, but the detectives who stopped by my office yesterday are still too involved in the case for me to step away without looking suspicious. We all need to lie low until I'm certain we're no longer considered suspects. No matter what happens, we need to stick to the same story and keep pushing the blame on Jonas."

"Are you kidding me?" Victor said. "Do you know how much money we'll all lose if we stop now?"

"How much *you'll* lose? You were nothing before you came to work for me, a drug addict making minimum wage. I made you who you are, and you've been rewarded handsomely for it. You're not in charge, and this isn't up for debate. All side business stops until I say otherwise."

"What are we supposed to do in the meantime?"

"Take some time off, take a vacation. You could all use one."

"You expect us to sit around with no pay?" Victor asked. "Just because it works for you doesn't mean it works for us."

"This won't last forever. In the meantime, I'll offer some compensation."

"How much?"

"I'll give you enough to help you make it through this time. Once things calm down, we'll get back on track."

Victor swished a hand through the air, rejecting the offer. "Naw. I'm not interested in chump change. After all we've done for you, we deserve better."

Max clenched his jaw.

Victor was younger than the others and a loose cannon with no respect for authority. Max blamed himself for not realizing it sooner. The kid had talent. He also had a severe case of PTSD.

Max had believed, at least for a while, that he could help Victor the way he'd helped Adam, by talking him down, getting inside his head, finding a way to fix whatever was broken. But Victor wasn't like Adam. He was unpredictable, defiant, and volatile. The more Max tried to reason with him, the more resistance he met.

Two of his men had already been taken out, disposed of in the last few weeks when they'd crossed a line they shouldn't have. Their disappearances had sent ripples of fear through the rest of the crew, and Max knew that adding Victor to the list would send the wrong message. Fear kept men obedient, but too much of it killed loyalty.

He leaned back, weighing the cost. If he eliminated Victor, he'd protect his operation in the short term, but he'd also risk losing the fragile control he still had. It was a risk he couldn't afford to take.

"The reason we're in this mess is because you botched the job with Juliette," Max snapped. "I told you both—no evidence, nothing traceable. But you left the body, you left the car. You ran her off the road and then abandoned her like amateurs. You went against everything you were trained to do. Everything that's happened since is the ripple effect of *your* mistake."

"My mistake?" Victor shot back, his voice rising. "You mean *your* girlfriend deciding to walk out on you and us scrambling to clean up the mess when she did. You told Jonas to take care of her. Not me. If he hadn't lost his nerve, I wouldn't have had to step in and finish the job myself."

"Take it easy, Victor," Adam said.

But Victor leaned in closer, his eyes burning with defiance. "I did what needed to be done. She's dead, and you've got the kid. Mission accomplished. If you're looking for someone to blame, maybe start with yourself. You're the one who dragged Juliette into this world of yours. What did you think was going to happen?"

A muscle twitched at Max's temple, a telltale sign that his temper was slipping. It always started that way, an involuntary pulse, a warning of what was coming. He hated when it happened, hated the heat that flooded his chest and the chaos that followed. When the anger took over, reason disappeared, and control was no longer an option.

"That's enough," Adam said. "Show some respect."

Infuriated, Victor gave Adam the bird, then turned his attention back to Max. "Your whole operation is falling apart. And don't think we all don't know about Trevor and Jonas and how you took them both out."

"I don't have to justify my actions to you," Max said.

Victor bolted out of his chair. "Trevor was my friend. He didn't need to die. I'm outta here."

"Sit back down," Max ordered.

"Naw, I'm leaving. Deal with it."

"Max told you to sit, Victor," Adam said.

"Screw you, Adam. Screw all of you."

Adam shot to his feet, grabbing Victor by the throat and slamming him against the wall. His fingers tightened, knuckles whitening as Victor struggled beneath his grip.

"You're young and stupid," Adam hissed. "Too stupid to recognize a good thing when it's staring you in the face."

Victor gagged, clawing at Adam's hands as he fought to pry them from his throat. But it was useless. Adam was bigger, stronger, and more experienced.

"Thank you, Adam," Max said. "I believe he's learned his lesson. You can let him go."

Adam released the pressure to Victor's neck but kept him pinned against the wall. "You listen to me, you little prick. You've compromised us all. We put our lives on the line to cover for you. If you don't want to be a team player anymore, say the word."

Victor glared at Max, who held his gaze, hoping the kid would cool his temper.

"I'm sorry," Victor said. "It won't happen again."

44

Max lingered in the doorway of Nora's bedroom, the dim light from the hallway stretching across the floor to where she slept. Her small form was curled beneath the blanket, her face peaceful one moment, then tightening the next as her breath quickened and a faint whimper escaped her lips. Each sound cut through him like glass. She was dreaming, and somewhere in those dreams, she was reliving everything he wished she could forget.

He wasn't a man easily shaken. But watching her now, fragile and broken by what she'd experienced, he felt something close to it. The weight of it pressed on his chest, unwelcome and suffocating.

He'd done this to her.

The fear in her eyes.

The restless sleep.

It all came back to him.

Standing there, he made himself a promise. He'd give her a new life, something brighter and better than what she had before. In time, she'd forget. He had to believe it. And when she did, things would be right again.

Nora's eyes fluttered open, and she turned, shaking as she saw him in the doorway.

"Hi, sweetie," Max said. "It's okay. You're with me now, and you're safe. Everything is going to be all right."

She stared at him for a time, then said, "The bad man hurt Mommy."

He crossed the room, sat beside her on the bed, and ran his hand through her hair. "The bad man is gone. You'll never see him again. I promise."

"I want my mommy and daddy."

It pained him not to be able to give her what she wanted, to know he couldn't because he was the one who was responsible for taking them from her.

"Did you know that sometimes little girls like you are so lucky they get to have more than one daddy?" he said.

She eyed him, curious and confused, but said nothing.

"Remember when we used to go to the park with Mommy?" he said. "Mommy told me if she ever had to go away one day, she wanted me to be your daddy. She wanted me to take care of you."

"Where is Mommy?"

There was no good answer to the question. "How about this? Tomorrow you Aunt Sasha will take you to the farmhouse to pet the horses. Would you like that?"

"I want to see Mommy."

He sighed. He had thought he could reason with her, but he was wrong. It was too soon. And though he lacked patience, patience was what Nora needed right now, and he had to find a way to give it to her.

Bending down, he kissed her on the forehead. "Let's talk about it in the morning, okay? Now it's time to sleep. Good-night, sweetheart."

45

F*ord*

Ford hadn't felt anything real for a woman in years. The job had hardened him, and grief had finished the rest. But the more time he spent with Raine, the more difficult it became to ignore his feelings. There was something magnetic about her, a spark that refused to be dimmed. Her sharp wit kept him on his toes, and her fearless determination reminded him of who he used to be before the losses started piling up.

Still, he knew better.

Acting on his feelings now would be wrong.

The case came first, and Raine deserved space to grieve before anything else. He'd wait until the investigation was over, until the dust had settled and the wounds weren't so raw. Whether she might ever feel the same way was a question he couldn't answer yet, but he hoped one day he would.

His thoughts drifted to Alisa, the last woman he'd loved,

and the only one who had ever known him. They'd lived together for seven years before the diagnosis came. Breast cancer. By the time it was found, it was already too late. Four months later, she was gone. Just like that.

After the funeral, Ford had unraveled. He took a leave from work, locked himself inside his house, and drowned himself in whiskey until it all ran dry, a handful of bottles of quiet destruction. Once they were gone, and he dragged himself out to stock back up on liquor, he'd driven past Songbird Gardens, the park where he and Alisa had spent so many weekends together. He pulled over and sat there, staring at the trees swaying in the wind, reflecting on old memories.

In that moment, he thought about what Alisa would see in him if she were still alive. A man broken, unshaven, hollowed out by loss. The night before she died, she'd made him promise to keep living, to find someone new, to not let grief take the rest of his life as it had taken hers.

He hadn't kept that promise.

Watching her fade had done something to him. It had closed a door he never thought could reopen. Even the idea of loving someone again felt dangerous. Love meant risk, and risk meant loss. He couldn't go through that a second time. So, he'd turned the car around, gone home, and buried himself in work, in Sherlock, his golden retriever, and in the handful of people who had remained close enough to care.

Now, Ford realized just how long he'd kept the world out, his heart locked behind a wall built out of fear and pain. Then came Raine, a light breaking through the cracks, steady and warm, reminding him of everything he thought he'd lost. Maybe, just maybe, it was time to open the window and let the sun back in.

46

R *aine*

It was morning, and Seth was now officially listed as a missing person. After their search the night before turned up nothing, they'd returned to Seth's house. Ford stretched out on the couch while Raine sat in the bathtub, trying to make sense of how everything in her life had fallen apart so fast.

A few minutes earlier, she'd called Anne, relieved to hear she was safe, even though they both agreed whatever was happening wasn't finished. Ford and Whitaker felt it too, and they'd advised Anne to stay put until things calmed, if they ever did.

Raine pulled on one of Juliette's shirts, which carried the faint scent of her sister's perfume, and then she gathered her hair into a loose bun. The smell of bacon drifted down the hall, leading her to the kitchen. Ford stood at the stove, still in yesterday's shirt, flipping an omelet onto a plate. When he saw Raine, he held it out to her.

"I appreciate it," Raine said, though I'm not sure I can eat."

"I haven't seen you touch anything since yesterday." He set the plate down, grabbed another, and took a forkful, nodding in approval. "It's good. Try it. A few bites won't hurt."

He wasn't wrong.

Raine had spent the last twenty-four hours running on coffee and grief, neither of which did much to keep her steady. She took the plate and sat at the table. The first few bites went down rough, but after a few more mouthfuls, she realized food was what she'd needed all along.

"Thank you," she said. "I've been thinking. I'd like to go somewhere."

He looked over at her. "Where?"

"There's someone I need to see, a relative I haven't visited in a while. She's in a rest home."

"When would you like to visit?"

"As soon as we've finished eating."

He paused, then said, "I'd like to come with you."

"Since you said you weren't letting me out of your sight, I assumed you would."

Raine hadn't counted on Ford staying close, but she was thankful he had. He seemed to grasp her need for seeing family, even if the only family left was an aunt who no longer remembered her name.

47

Aunt Cora sat in a recliner near the window, wrapped in a blue robe with matching slippers. Outside, two birds perched on a branch, their soft songs drifting through the glass. The television played an old episode of *Murder, She Wrote*, a show they used to watch together when Raine was young and spent weekends at her house.

A book rested open on Cora's lap, upside down, forgotten.

When Raine stepped into the room, she turned her head and smiled. For a moment, it was like time hadn't touched her. Her hair was still the same silvery shade she remembered, her eyes still bright. She held Raine's gaze, and silence filled the space between them. Raine tried to speak, to say *hello*, but the word stuck in her throat. It had been too long since she'd come to see her, and standing there now, the weight of that neglect was heavy.

"What's the matter, sweetie?" Cora said. "Are you okay?"

Raine shook her head.

"Well, why not? What's wrong?"

Everything.

Everything is wrong.

"I'm sorry I haven't been here to see you in such a long time," Raine said.

Cora turned, focusing on Ford. "And who's come to visit me today?"

"Ma'am," he said. "I'm a friend of your niece. It's nice to meet you."

She blushed, glanced at the upside-down page in her book, and then looked at Raine again. "I'm sorry. What did you just say?"

"I'm Raine, your niece. Do you remember me?"

Of course she didn't.

Still, Raine hesitated, thinking if she stared at her long enough, something inside would spark her sense of recognition.

"Raine. What a nice name. It reminds me of the sky, but not on a day as beautiful as today."

Ford grabbed a couple of chairs from the table, and they sat beside her.

Raine folded her hand inside hers and said, "Before I was born, you helped my mother decide what to name me. You liked Raine because it made you think of the day my mother told you she was pregnant with me as the two of you sat on the porch during a thunderstorm."

She nodded. "If you say so, dear."

"Remember Juliette? She visited you all the time. I bet she brought Nora with her too."

Cora's gaze drifted toward the window. "Did you bring pecan pie? I like pecan pie. I have one slice every day. Never two. Two makes my stomach hurt. But one slice is just right."

"I can go see what they have in the cafeteria if you like," Ford offered.

"Oh, no. The lady in the white pants brings it. What's her

name again? I think it starts with an H. Helen or Heather or Hattie or ..."

Ford's phone buzzed, and he stood. "I'm going to take this in the hall, give you two some time to catch up."

Raine nodded, and he stepped out.

"I need to talk to you about something," Raine said.

Or try to talk to her, at least.

"I hear you just fine," she said. "What is it?"

"Juliette won't be able to visit you anymore."

"Sure, she will. She comes on Thursday. What day is today?"

Today.

Today was Thursday.

"What I mean to say is, Juliette was in a car crash a few days ago, and she died," Raine said. "I'm sorry. I know how close you were."

"A car crash? Were Thomas and Laura there, too?"

Thomas and Laura were Raine's parents.

Cora had made a connection.

"Thomas and Laura died a long time ago," Raine said.

Cora cupped her hands to the sides of Raine's face. "Everybody's dead now? I can't believe it. We were all eating dinner together last week."

The change in Cora hit Raine harder than she expected and guilt settled deep in her chest for the second time that morning. She should have come sooner, should have been here for her the way Juliette always had.

"I'm still here," Raine said. "And I'm going to see about moving you to a place closer to me."

"Oh, that's nice. Will it have television?"

"I'll make sure of it."

They talked about ordinary things, their conversations circling back whenever Cora lost her train of thought. Each time it happened, Raine's heart sank a little more. She wanted to remember her as she'd been—energetic, sharp, full of spirit—not as the frail woman sitting across from her now.

Some time passed, and Raine kissed Cora on the cheek and stood. "I need to go now. I'll visit soon, okay?"

"Will we go to the new place next time?"

"I hope so."

Raine leaned in to hug Cora, and the book slipped from Cora's lap, landing on the floor with a soft thud. As she bent to pick it up, a necklace fell forward from beneath her robe. Raine gasped, realizing the necklace reminded her of another piece of jewelry, the bracelet she'd found in the pocket of Juliette's dress.

"Where did you get such a pretty necklace?" Raine asked.

Cora tipped her head, trying to get a good look at it. "What is it?"

"Here, I'll show you." Raine undid the clasp and flattened the necklace on her hand. "Did Juliette give this to you?"

Cora looked confused. "I don't know."

Raine pulled out her phone, flipping through her photos until she found one of Juliette. She showed it to her. "This is Juliette. Did she give you the necklace?"

She stared at Juliette's photo. "She's pretty, isn't she? Pretty like you."

Raine sighed, knowing it was unreasonable for her to think Cora would be able to answer her question. "It's okay. Don't worry about it. I'll put the necklace back on you now."

"The pretty girl said I could borrow it. When she visits again, I have to give it back. Then she lets me borrow something new. I take it off each night before bed and keep it in the box."

"What box?"

Cora turned her head, pointing toward the bedroom.

Raine stepped inside and paused, taking in the simplicity of the space. There was a bed, a nightstand, and a dresser along the far wall. The top drawer was open, and she walked to it, looking in. Beside a couple of nightgowns, was a small, elegant gold box. She picked it up and lifted the lid. On the underside, written in pen, were the words: *To My Sweet Juliette, Yours Always, Max.*

48

Raine closed the bedroom door behind her and sat on the edge of Cora's bed, her hands trembling as she dialed Anne's number.

"Hey, how are things going with you today?" Anne asked.

"It's been an interesting morning."

"Oh?"

"How well do you know Max?"

"I've met him a few times. He's a nice man. Why?"

Raine drew in a slow breath, trying to steady her voice. "I need to speak with him. Do you know where he lives?"

"Why? What's going on?"

"I'll explain later, I promise."

"Raine, what did you find out?"

"Maybe nothing. Maybe something. I'm not sure yet. What's he like?"

Anne hesitated. "Wealthy. Sophisticated. Handsome. The kind of man who makes you feel like he's always two steps ahead, like he's figured you out before you've even said a word about yourself."

It struck Raine how different he sounded from Seth. If Juliette had been searching for more in her life—excitement, power, something beyond the ordinary—Max's charm and confidence could have been what drew her in.

"I think Max knew Juliette," Raine said.

"How would he?"

"I don't know. But if you give me his address, I'll find out."

"I'm not sure of his exact address, but once I was driving around with Jonas, and we passed by a gated community. Inside were a handful of some of the biggest villas I'd ever seen. Jonas pointed them out and said Max lived inside in the biggest house at the end. I think they were called Evergreen or Everwood."

Everwood Point, the most sought-after estate villas in the city.

"Is he married?" Raine asked. "Any kids?"

"From what Jonas told me, he's single, and I've never seen him with a woman, which always surprised me. It always seemed like women were drawn to him, but he's always struck me as the type of person who never lets anyone get too close."

"Got it. Thanks for the information. I'll catch up with you later."

The call ended, and Raine sat there for a long moment, the silence pressing in around her. For the first time in days, she felt something other than dread. She felt hope. Hope that Max might be the missing piece, the key to understanding what had happened to Nora and to Juliette and why.

49

Max's Italian-style villa sat tucked away from the road, shrouded in the kind of privacy only wealth could buy. Mature oaks and cypress trees flanked the long drive, their branches reaching across one another like outstretched arms, blocking most of the house from view. The wrought-iron gate at the entrance was open, an unsettling detail in a neighborhood where every other gate they'd passed had been closed and locked tight.

Raine hesitated as they drove through, the tires crunching against the gravel as Ford followed the winding path toward the house. The villa came into view piece by piece—a terracotta roof, cream stucco walls. It was beautiful, in a kind of old-world way.

The front door stood slightly ajar, suggesting someone hadn't shut it all the way, or someone had left in a hurry. That, combined with the fact that the gate had been left open, gave Raine a sense of unease.

Ford parked and glanced over at Raine, who sat beside him, his eyes narrowing as he scanned the entryway. He didn't say anything, but she could tell he was thinking the same thing she had.

Something about this scene wasn't right.

"I'm still not sure I should have brought you here," he said.

"There's no way I wasn't going to be part of it, not after all I've been through."

"Yeah ... well, for now, I want you to stay here."

Raine stepped out of the car. "No way. I'm coming with you."

"Raine, please. At least let me check things out first."

She slid back onto the seat but kept the door cracked open, one foot still on the gravel, doing her best to resist following him.

Through the windshield, she watched Ford disappear through the front door.

She was a bit shocked he'd let himself in, given she knew he could get himself in trouble for it if Max made a fuss.

One minute passed.

Then two.

Still nothing.

The longer Raine sat there, the heavier the quiet became, pressing against her until she couldn't sit there anymore.

She reached for the gun, tucked it into the waistband of her jeans, and stepped out. When she reached the front door, she leaned in, just enough to get a view of the entryway.

"Ford?" she whispered.

She heard no one, saw no one.

She stepped inside, her gaze landing on a marble floor and up a sweeping staircase. A moment later, the deep, hollow chime of a grandfather clock rang out from somewhere in the next room.

She moved through the main floor, passing through one

immaculate room after another. The living area was staged like it was straight out of a design magazine with leather furniture and framed art. It felt less like a home and more like a show-room, a space meant to impress rather than live in.

At the base of the staircase, she paused, listening. There was no sound of movement above. She took her time climbing the steps, one hand on the railing, the other palming her gun.

At the end of the hall, she pushed open the door to the master bedroom. Darkness greeted her, thick and unmoving. She flipped the switch, flooding the space with soft light. The room was pristine, not a single thing out of place.

Continuing her quiet search, she found three more bedrooms along the upstairs hall. The first two were identical guest rooms in neutral tones and untouched linens, not a single personal belonging in sight. When she reached the third door at the end of the corridor, she noticed it was closed, unlike the others.

She wrapped her hand around the knob and turned it, the hinges protesting with a soft creak as the door opened a few inches to peek inside.

The room was different than all the rest. The bed was unmade, and a comforter draped halfway off the mattress, pooling across the carpet. Pastel art hung on the walls, and a small wooden dollhouse sat beneath the window.

Everything about it told Raine it was a little girl's room.

But how could it be?

Anne had told her Max didn't have children.

So, whose room was it?

Raine nudged the door open the rest of the way, and that's when she saw her. A woman lay sprawled on the carpet, motionless, her skin pale against the dark red stain spreading beneath her.

Raine pressed a hand to her lips and rushed over.

Reaching down, she felt for a pulse.

There wasn't one.

The woman was dead.

50

The woman on the floor looked to be in her fifties, and she was at least twice Raine's size. She lay curled onto her side, knees drawn in, one hand pressed to her neck as if she'd tried to protect herself in the final moments of her life.

Raine crouched beside her, the carpet damp beneath her knee as she studied the woman's face. The woman's skin had lost all color, and her eyes were half-open and glassy. The faint smell of gunpowder still lingered in the air, sharp and metallic.

Raine leaned a bit closer, scanning for a wound. It didn't take long to find one. She'd been shot once, the bullet's entry point just above her right temple.

Who was this woman?

What was she doing in a child's room in Max's house?

Why had someone killed her?

And *where* was Ford?

Raine's gaze caught on something small, a thin, pink headband sticking out of the pocket of a child's pair of pants. She reached down and pulled it free, the fabric familiar as she rubbed it between her fingers.

She'd seen the headband before.

It was Nora's.

Raine's instincts had been right to come here.

She stepped back from the doorway, her mind spinning as the reality of what she'd just walked into sank in. Backing into the hallway, she just stood there for a moment, trying to decide what to do next.

Movement was heard on the stairs.

Someone was coming.

She raised her gun and waited.

A shadow shifted on the wall, then a man appeared.

"Stop right there," Raine said.

The man steadied himself, curling a hand around the banister. "There's no need to point a gun. This is my house. You're the one who's trespassing."

"You're Max."

"And you must be Raine," he said, nodding. "I assume you came here to talk, which I'm willing to do *if* you put the gun down."

"You'll talk either way."

His hand darted beneath his shirt, and instinct took over, as Raine's eyes landed on the gun he was carrying.

She squeezed the trigger.

The shot cracked through the hallway, lodging into the wall behind him. She'd meant to graze him, just enough to stop him if he was pulling on him, and she missed, something she didn't do often.

The mistake cost her.

By the time the ringing in her ears began to fade, his gun was trained on her.

"Lower your weapon and back against the wall," he said.

She shook her head, preparing to fire again.

"Don't even think about taking another shot," he said. "Not

unless you want to die. Unlike your failed attempt, I never miss."

If Raine did what he wanted, she was dead anyway.

Before she had the chance to decide, a sharp pain ripped through her chest. She looked down, realizing he'd returned fire, the bullet having struck just above her right breast.

"That was a warning," he said. "Drop the gun, or I'll fire again."

"You'll fire either way. If I keep my gun on you, at least I have a fighting chance."

He laughed as though he found her amusing. "You know something? I'm glad we met. You remind me of your sister, except you're a whole lot feistier."

"The sister you murdered?"

"I didn't murder her."

"You may not have driven the car that ran her off the road, but you were involved, weren't you?"

"I loved your sister."

"Juliette, Jonas Parr, and I'm guessing Sadie Tucker—all dead. And who knows how many others. I don't believe a man like you understands the meaning of love."

Raine had missed once, but if she steadied her nerves, she could correct that mistake the next time she fired. Under normal circumstances, her aim never faltered. Even if they both pulled the trigger at the same moment, she trusted her shot to land where she intended in the chaos of the crossfire.

Keeping his eyes fixed on my gun, he said, "Looks like we're at an impasse. I won't fire again if you agree to do the same. At least not until you get the answers you're after. That *is* why you're here, isn't it?"

Raine nodded in agreement, using her free hand to remove the jewelry box in her pocket. She tossed it in his direction. It hit his chest and then fell to the floor and sprung open. He glanced down at it, at the words he'd written, then back at her.

"Did you give the necklace that was in that box to my sister?" Raine asked.

"I did."

"Why?"

"We were in love."

"There's no need to lie to me," she said.

"I'm not."

"Why did you have her killed?"

"The simple answer to your question is that she saw something she wasn't supposed to see."

"And that was reason enough for you to end her life?"

"I know it's difficult to believe, but I wanted a life with your sister, no matter how unconventional it appeared. She was told to stay silent about what she saw, told not to run. When she defied me, she left me with no choice."

"You had a choice. There's *always* a choice."

"You and I have different morals. Call me a killer if it makes you feel better."

"Where's Nora?"

He smiled as if enjoying the conversation. "It must be so disappointing."

"Which part?"

"You broke into my house to save your niece, only to discover she's not here."

"Your front door was open when I arrived."

He shook his head, indicating he didn't believe her.

"I've been in the pool house all morning. And I can assure you; the doors are always locked in my absence."

"If they're locked, how did *I* get in?"

He narrowed his eyes, indicating she had a point, then he

shifted his gaze upward, and Raine noticed a surveillance camera.

"Interesting," he said.

"What's interesting?"

"It would appear my surveillance cameras have been shut off. I assume you had something to do with it."

"I didn't. I couldn't care less about your surveillance. I want to know if my niece is alive."

"She is, yes."

It was the admission she'd been waiting for, the one she'd stopped believing would come. Her pulse quickened as the truth settled in. Nora was alive. She wanted to collapse beneath the weight of Max's revelation, but the gun in his hand kept her still.

"Why did you take her?"

"Why indeed. Have you ever noticed she doesn't look a thing like Seth?"

Raine drew in a breath and took a step back, her gaze sweeping over him with new understanding. The resemblance was undeniable. Nora's narrow eyes, the curve of her nose, even the faint crease that formed when she frowned. All of it was his.

"You're her father."

"I am."

Raine's chest tightened, a mixture of rage and grief. She wanted to recoil, to deny it outright, but the truth clung to her, raw and unrelenting. It didn't matter that Juliette had never admitted the truth. Biology had written his name across her face, and Raine hated that it changed everything—how she saw him, how she saw Juliette.

"Where is Nora?" Raine asked.

"She's spending the day with my sister."

His *sister*. "When's the last time you spoke to your sister?"

He eyed her like the question troubled him. "Why do you ask?"

"Does your sister have a one-inch birthmark beneath her left ear?"

"What are you getting at?"

Raine reached out, pushing the bedroom door open. "It looks like your sister is here. But if she's here, *where's* Nora?"

51

Max raced into the bedroom, dropping to his knees as if the world had folded beneath him. He pulled his sister into his arms, holding her like a child.

He glared at Raine, eyes hollow. "I'll kill you for what you've done!"

And it occurred to Raine that Max was blaming her for his sister's death.

"I had nothing to do with what happened to your sister," Raine said. "She was dead when I got here."

He pushed away from the body and stared at Raine as if searching for some proof that she was lying. "Where's Nora? What have you done with her?"

"If I had her, do you think I would still be here, asking you the same question? I would be long gone."

As much as Raine was trying to keep it together, she was starting to panic. *Someone* had Nora, and it wasn't him.

"Don't play games with me," he said. "You wanted to even the score. I killed your sister, so you killed mine."

"You have it wrong," Raine said. "I didn't even know you had a sister before now."

"Yes, you did. You must have. You came here, and you waited until I was back in the house so you could see the look on my face when I realized what you'd done."

Raine's attention shifted from Max to something she hadn't noticed before, a note sitting on top of a pillow.

"Looks like someone left you a note," she said.

"What are you talking—"

He turned, snatching the paper off the pillow.

He read line after line, and for the first time Raine noticed something she hadn't before—real fear in his eyes.

"It can't be," he mumbled. "He wouldn't dare."

"Read it," Raine said. "Out loud."

"It's not for you," he said, clutching the paper to his chest. "I'll deal with this by myself."

"I said read it, or I'll put a bullet in your head."

He held her gaze a moment, then said, "No, you won't. If you shoot me, you will lose your only chance of ever seeing your niece again."

Max's tone told Raine he wasn't bluffing, his words landing like a fist to her gut. Even with her gun fixed on him, he still believed he had the upper hand. They stood locked in place, the air between them charged and unsteady. Raine didn't breathe, didn't blink. She waited for him to speak, to reveal what was written in the note. She'd come so close to reuniting with Nora, and yet she still felt so far.

52

There was commotion on the stairs, and Raine turned, relieved to see Ford.

He reached the bedroom, and she said, "Where have you been?"

"In the basement."

"Didn't you hear the gunshots?"

"I didn't. I'm guessing the whole house is soundproofed."

Ford's attention shifted to the dead woman, then to Max, and then to Raine's bloodstained shirt, and the gun she held in her hand.

"You've been shot," he said. "Are you all right?"

"I'll be fine. Right now, we have bigger problems."

"What's happened?"

She tipped her head toward Max. "He admitted he ordered my sister's murder, and then he claimed Nora was alive and with his sister. But his sister is the woman lying dead on the floor, and Nora's not here. I don't know where she is, or who took her. Someone left Max a note, and he refuses to read it."

"Did you—"

As if knowing what he was about to ask, Raine shook her head. "She was already dead when I got here."

Max began to speak, but Ford cut him off. "Shut your mouth. I'll deal with you next."

"You'll not speak to me like—"

"I can, and I will. Now shut up."

"Nora is alive," Raine said. "We have to find her."

In one swift motion, Ford struck Max's gun from his grip, the weapon clattering across the floor before sliding to a stop at Raine's feet. Max froze, his face in shock. As Raine crouched to retrieve it, Ford said, "We'll find her. But right now, I need you to lower your weapon."

Raine didn't want to lower her weapon.

She wanted to fire on Max until every bullet in the chamber was spent.

"Raine, I need you to listen to me," Ford said. "Max will get what he deserves. I promise."

He *promised*.

Over time, she'd learned to loathe the word.

She kept the gun on Max. "He *won't* get what he deserves. Even if he's convicted, he'll find a way to get out of it. Why does he get to live when my sister didn't?"

"Do as the man says," Max said with a grin.

Raine was tired of being told what to do.

She aimed at Max's leg and fired, and he curled over, gritting his teeth in pain. Seeing him struggle satisfied her. It just didn't satisfy her enough.

"Raine!" Ford yelled.

"All right, all right," she said. "I'll lower my weapon."

"Listen, I called for backup. They'll be here anytime."

Max shook his head, his tone sharp with sarcasm. "Perfect. Just what we need. More cops."

Ford ignored the comment, his attention turning to Raine as he pointed at the sister. "Did you examine her?"

"Just for a minute," Raine said. "She's in algor mortis. I'm guessing she was murdered in the last hour."

"Anything else?"

"I still don't know what is in the note someone left on the pillow." Raine pointed at Max. "*He* has it. It's in his pocket."

Ford snapped his fingers at Max. "Hand it over."

Max huffed an irritated sigh, then grabbed the note, balling it up in his hand and then tossing it to the ground in front of Ford. But Ford wasn't stupid, and he wasn't about to lower his weapon.

He turned toward Raine, saying, "Go on. Get it."

"You're wasting time," Max said. "Valuable time. Your involvement will only make things worse. If you want to see Nora again, you need to let me handle the situation myself."

Raine ignored the comment, opening the note and reading aloud.

Five million dollars.
  Eleven p.m. behind Carlotta's Diner.
  If you don't show, the brat dies.

Don't test me.
  V

Raine looked at Max. "Who's V?"

Max looked away, refusing to answer.

Ford slammed his fist into Max's face, the impact snapping

his head to the side. "Now isn't the time to stay silent. Answer the question."

Max spit a mouthful of blood onto the floor, saying nothing.

"I'll put another bullet in you if I have to, but you *will* tell me," Ford said.

Max let out a bitter laugh. "You're a real piece of work, Detective. The first time we met, I thought you were different, a man with morals, with decency. Someone who'd uphold the law even if it meant watching every member of your family die right before your eyes. But now? Now I see a bully. No better than every other corrupt cop I've ever met."

Ford leaned in close, his voice low and gritty. "Why is Nora worth so much to you? Why take her in the first place? Whatever you started here, whatever game you've been playing—it's over."

"Neither of you understands. Every minute you waste waiting and failing to chase this man costs us time. I know him. He meant what he wrote in that note. He will kill Nora unless we stop him. None of us wants that."

"You're the one who doesn't understand," Ford said. "Whitaker called me this morning. Your associate, Adam Chase, is in custody. Turns out he left his DNA behind while cleaning up your mess at Sadie Tucker's house. Seems to me your entire operation is falling apart."

"You're lying."

Ford shrugged. "Believe me or don't. When the police arrive and you're in cuffs, we'll see how much loyalty your people still have for you. If you think Adam won't sell you out to save his own skin, you have another thing coming."

53

dam

Adam was in serious trouble.

After killing Sadie a few nights earlier, he'd gone into the bedroom to grab Nora, and in his rush to keep her quiet, his head struck the bedpost with a sharp crack. He hadn't realized at the time that the sting he felt wasn't just from the impact. He'd torn out several strands of hair in the process.

Now he sat in an interrogation room at the police department across from Detective Whitaker, accused of Sadie's murder and being pressed for answers about Nora and Seth. They would never find Sadie's body. But knowing the police had proof he'd been in her house the same day Nora was there made his stomach turn.

It also made him question what else they knew.

Unsure where to turn, he faced a choice he'd never imagined making. Max had been everything to him. He was his mentor, the closest thing to family he'd ever known. Turning against him was a betrayal. But what other choice did he have?

Max had stepped in at Adam's lowest point when his dishonorable discharge left him hollow and teetering on the edge. He'd pulled Adam back from the darkness, giving him purpose when he had none. And now, to save himself, Adam was about to destroy the only man who had ever believed in him.

A forensics expert entered the room, a woman who introduced herself as Sarah Dixon.

"Hair collected at Sadie Tucker's crime scene contained follicular tissue, which allowed me to create a unique DNA profile," she said. "When we test it against the strands we collected from you today, we're confident it will be a match."

And that wasn't all they had on him.

An oddly placed surveillance camera at the community's entrance caught a fuzzy image of Adam carrying something small wrapped in a blanket to the car. A minute later, a second blanket was seen being hauled out of the condo. It was much larger and lumpier, a gross oversight on Adam's part. He'd disabled two of the cameras but had failed to see the third. He wasn't the kind of man who made careless mistakes. He blamed it on the mounting pressure, on how everything had spiraled out of control since Juliette's death. No time to plan, to prepare. He'd gotten sloppy.

"We're not interested in you," Whitaker said. "And I'm sure you know that already. You're the small fish. We want the big one."

"Meaning?"

"You fill in the blanks, and we'll make you a deal." Whitaker leaned in, his breath thick with the bitter scent of old coffee. "Refuse, and I'll see to it you're charged for every murder that's gone down this week related to this case—body or no body."

Adam wanted to believe Max wouldn't allow it to happen. But Max was losing his cool, making rash decisions, allowing his own personal feelings to cloud his otherwise impeccable judgment.

Two of Adam's coworkers had been slain in less than a month, which caused him to question their entire operation.

"What's it going to be?" Whitaker pressed.

"I'm not talking."

"All right, then. I'll let you mull my offer over while we talk about something else." Whitaker tossed a plastic evidence bag in Adam's direction. The bag contained a black card. "We found this business card in your possession when we picked you up. We'd like you to explain it."

Adam shrugged.

"You know what's interesting?" Whitaker said. "Jonas Parr had a small stack of these same business cards tucked away in a hidden compartment beneath the seat of his car."

"It doesn't mean anything. We worked together, so it makes sense we'd have the same cards."

"What I want to know is what else you two were mixed up in," Whitaker said. "Because I called the number on that card. You want to know what happened? A man answered. He asked me for a password. I had no idea what he was talking about, and when I didn't respond fast enough, he hung up. I tried calling back five minutes later, but the line was dead. Strange, don't you think?"

Adam shrugged.

"Seth's world is collapsing around him," Whitaker said. "If you refuse to talk, he'll take you and everyone else who works for him along for the ride. And you know something? Most rides don't last long in prison. Maybe you'll get lucky, or maybe you'll wind up dead. Either way, you'll wish you were. Are you a gambling man?"

Adam leaned back in his chair. "I know how this works. Everything is fine with Max. I talked to him this morning. Nice try, though."

"How long has it been since that phone call?"

"Why?"

"Max's sister was found dead inside his home this morning."

Adam could feel himself starting to panic.

Whitaker was bluffing.

There was no way what he was saying was true.

Was there?

"Someone shot his sister," Whitaker continued. "And you know what else? The Granger girl, Nora, the one everyone assumed Jonas Parr had buried somewhere. It turns out she may be alive, after all."

"What makes you think she's alive?"

"For starters, when you abducted her from Sadie Tucker's house, which I'm assuming you did, you missed something— Nora's stuffed animal under the bed. Explain to me how her stuffed animal ended up in Sadie Tucker's condo. A condo *you've* been in."

"Don't ask me. Ask Jonas. Oh, wait. You can't. He's dead."

"Think you're funny, huh? I'm not done. Today, in the room where Max's sister was found dead, a ransom note had been left on the bed. Money in exchange for the girl. Tell me this, why would anyone demand payment for a child who's dead?"

Adam tried to swallow, but his mouth was dry, his tongue thick and useless, refusing to summon even a trace of moisture.

Whitaker grinned as if pleased with himself. "Can I get you something? Water? Soda? Coffee? Lie detector test?"

"What else did the ransom note say?"

"Max is to meet tonight behind Carlotta's Diner with five

million dollars. If he doesn't show, Nora dies. The note was signed with a single initial. V."

Victor, he thought.

Adam hung his head, raking his fingers through his hair.

How did something so good go so wrong so fast?

"We're running out of time to save this girl, Adam," Whitaker said. "Make your decision, or I'll pull my offer right now."

The escalation of events had happened so fast, Adam couldn't even think straight. As much as he wanted to save Max, he needed to save himself. "I tell you, and I get no prison time?"

"Let me ask you this—did your employer order every crime you carried out?"

Adam glanced up at the tiny red light below the room's surveillance camera. "Off the record until I see the deal."

Whitaker shifted his gaze to the tinted glass across the room and motioned toward it with a sweeping wave of his hand. A moment later, the light behind the window flicked off. "We've done what you asked. Now it's your turn."

"The answer is yes," Adam whispered. "I was paid. If that affects my deal, I'll deny ever saying it, and we have nothing left to talk about."

"I believe we can work something out. Can't say you won't do *any* time, but if you're not willing to help, you're looking at a life sentence."

"Just so we're clear, I'll only disclose the events that occurred around Juliette's death. And if I do go to prison, I'll need to be in the Witness Protection Program when I get out. I'll be a target. Max or one of our former clients will find a way to come after me."

Whitaker nodded. "Understood. I'll check with my superior, but I believe we have ourselves a deal."

54

F*ord*

Whitaker and Ford sat in the interrogation room across from Max.

Rattling Max would be easy.

Getting him to confess, not so much.

"Tell me about the side business, Max," Ford asked.

Max paused, then said, "There is no side business."

Ford exchanged glances with Whitaker.

"So, you don't run a murder-for-hire business using a handful of dishonorably discharged military snipers?" Ford asked.

"Sounds like an interesting business. But no."

Whitaker grabbed the black business card, holding it between two fingers. "I was told that if I dialed the number and said 'brugad,' a meeting would be arranged where payment is secured for killing whoever the client wants dead."

"I wouldn't know anything about it. I'm in the investment business."

"Brugad." Whitaker tapped the card. "Odd word, isn't it? You know what it means. It's mob-speak for family."

A smug, unimpressed Max leaned back in his chair. "Why don't we dial the number listed on the card and see what happens?"

"Oh, I have. Problem is, it's out of service now, unlike the first time I called when a man answered and then hung up when I didn't know the password."

"My lawyer will be here in no time. Until then, I must insist you don't ask any further questions."

Whitaker removed a small tape recorder from his pocket. "I'd like to play something for you, if you don't mind. Hell, I'll play it for you even if you *do* mind."

He placed the recorder on the table and pressed play, and Adam's voice streamed through the speaker.

"I started working for Max Duran six years ago, not long after the military let me go. He gave me an investment position at his company while he groomed me to work for a different side of the business that he'd started."

"What business is that?"

"Murder for hire."

"Turn it off," Max said. "He's only saying what you want to hear because you bullied him into a false confession. Happens all the time."

The tape played on with Adam explaining how the business worked and how the deals were made. And then the conversation turned to Juliette.

"What was Juliette Granger's relationship to Max?"

"She was his girlfriend."

"For how long?"

"I don't know. Few years, I guess."

"Why was she murdered?"

"She witnessed him kill another man. After, he worried she'd run, and so he had us all take turns tailing her in case she did. It was a pain, to be honest. We sat down the street from her place day and night, just sitting. It got old real fast. I thought he was being paranoid. But I also knew if she ran, she was a dead woman."

"Who killed her?"

"Victor. Jonas was also there. He was supposed to do it himself. He couldn't, so he had Victor do it instead, which was how everything got screwed up in the first place."

"And Nora ... what happened to her?"

"She was removed from Juliette's car before the car went over the ledge. Jonas was supposed to deliver her to Max when he got back that day, but he didn't."

"Why not?"

"I don't know. He took her to Sadie Tucker's house, thinking no one would know she was there. Max knew, though. He knows everything. He's always watching."

"Who killed Jonas?"

"Max."

"Where's Seth Granger?"

"Dead."

"How do you know? Did you kill him?"

"I didn't, but I picked him up at the bar and dropped him off at Max's house. Several hours later, Max texted me to call the cleaner."

"Are you willing to testify to all of this in court?"

"If I'm protected—yes."

Whitaker stopped the tape.

"Your associate goes on, of course, but I think you've heard enough." He waved a hand toward the door, and two armed police officers walked in. "These two officers will escort you to holding while you wait for your lawyer. It's a good thing he's coming. The sooner the better, I say."

55

R *aine*

Raine was sitting in the passenger seat of Ford's vehicle. He'd refused to bring her along at first but then changed his mind after deciding Nora had been through enough. She deserved to see a familiar face when they found her, the face of a person she knew and trusted. Someone who made her feel safe.

Raine had been given strict instructions to remain in the car when they arrived, which she agreed to do—for now.

The plan was simple.

Using Max's cell phone, a text had been sent to Victor saying Adam would be there to hand the money over in exchange for Nora. Adam rebuffed the idea at first, until he was reminded that his cooperation in Nora's rescue was part of the deal he'd made with the police.

Ford parked just far enough away from the meeting place and switched the car off. "Earlier, I thought it would be best for you to stay in the truck. But now that we're here, and we don't know what this Victor guy will do, I think you should be with me. If I let you tag along, I need you to do whatever I tell you, all right?"

Raine nodded.

He waited for the SWAT team to arrive and then they exited the vehicle. The armed men filed out, disappearing into the night. Seconds later, Whitaker walked past, with Adam by his side.

Five minutes passed, then ten.

They heard nothing, saw nothing.

After fifteen minutes, they moved toward the restaurant, guided only by a faint, flickering light near the entrance. Raine caught the sound of raised voices cutting through the quiet and edged along the side of the building, the rough brick scraping her shoulder as they slid forward until they reached the corner.

Two men stood in the alleyway, guns drawn.

"You're twenty minutes late, Victor."

"Where's Max?"

"You knew he wouldn't be here."

Victor scanned the area. "Come on out, Max. I know you're here."

"I told you. He sent me. I'm alone."

"And here I thought he'd show up and try to kill me. Where's the money?"

"Where's Nora?"

"She's close by."

"I need to see her."

"Money first."

"Kid first."

"Money, Adam. I won't ask again."

Adam opened a duffel bag and removed a stack of bills. "It's all here, just like you asked. You want it, you give me Nora. We both walk away. And if you want some unsolicited advice, I suggest you leave the country before Max comes for you."

Victor waved his gun in the air, laughing. "You're a funny guy, Adam. The minute I give her over to you, I'm a dead man. Max killed Trevor over nothing. I killed his only sibling. There's no chance he'll ever let me go."

Raine turned, looking at Ford who held a finger to his lips, indicating to keep quiet.

"So, how's this going to work?" Adam said. "You want the money, and I need to take Nora to Max. I don't know what else to say."

"Get him on the phone."

The suggestion took Adam by surprise. "Even if I call him, he won't talk to you."

"He'll talk to *you*, though, his favorite whipping boy."

Adam slung the duffel bag over his shoulder, took out his phone, dialed, and waited. "It's ringing. What do you want me to say?"

"Hand me the phone when he answers. I'll say it myself."

Adam paused, then said, "He didn't answer. Told you."

"He was willing to part with all this money to get the little brat back, and he can't take your call? Where is he?"

Max stepped into the alley, hands raised. "I'm right here, Victor, and I'm unarmed. You can check if you like."

"I do *like*." Victor walked over and patted Max down. "Why didn't you come out before?"

"I only just arrived. I sent Adam along ahead of me."

"I don't believe you."

"I don't care about the money. I can make more of it. The only thing that matters to me is Nora."

Victor pressed his gun to the center of Max's head. "Why? Why is she worth so much to you?"

"It doesn't concern you. Hand her over and go. And Victor, I *never* want to see you again. If you're stupid enough to stick around, consider yourself a dead man."

Victor grunted a laugh. "Go get the money from Adam."

Max hesitated a moment, then did what Victor asked.

"I'd like to see Nora," Max said.

Victor backed toward an abandoned building, his gaze fixed on Max and Adam. Jerking open the door, he reached in, yanking a frightened Nora out, his arm locked tight around her as he forced her forward.

The moment Raine laid eyes on her, her hands flew to her mouth, and she leaned into Ford to keep her knees from buckling beneath her.

At long late, here she was—filthy, trembling, and beautiful.

And alive.

Victor stopped a few feet in front of Max and said, "Toss me the bag."

Max tossed it over to him.

"Now let her go," Max said.

Max bent down, his arms open wide.

"Walk to Max," Victor said.

"It's okay, sweetheart," Max said, "You're safe now."

As Nora began to walk, Victor raised his gun and fired, the bullet striking Max in the center of his head, killing him. As the SWAT team moved in, Ford and Raine sprinted toward Nora. Raine reached her first and bent down, scooping her into her arms.

Shaking with terror, Nora clung to her. "Ree-Ree!"

Raine pressed a kiss to Nora's wet cheeks, running a hand through the child's hair as she said, "It's okay, sweetheart. Auntie Raine's here, and I'll always be."

56

R*aine*

One year later, Raine walked out of Willow Woods Nursing Home, clutching Nora's small hand in hers. Not long after she'd come to live with her, Raine had obtained legal guardianship of her niece. Then she returned to Las Vegas for Cora, settling her into an assisted living center close to her home.

Nora had battled the weight of trauma after losing her parents, most of which she had been processing through therapy. Some days were harder than others, but she was beginning to heal, finding her footing little by little. Being so young, Raine hoped some of the traumatic memories Nora endured had started to blur, but she made sure Juliette and Seth remained close to her heart. She kept them alive through stories and photos she'd placed around the house.

With Max dead, Raine assumed the deal Alex had struck had died with him. But Alex knew where the bodies were buried, including two in particular: Sadie Tucker and Raine's brother-in-law, Seth, who had died at Max's hand.

A new deal was offered to Adam, and with it a promise to shorten his prison sentence. For it, he agreed to provide the police with information on every burial sites he knew about as well as giving up the names of their clients. He'd balked at the deal at first, but once the idea of life behind bars without parole set in, he began to sing. And as to the alleged affair between Jonas and Juliette? He said it never happened.

Victor didn't fare as well as Adam, and for his part in everything, he was be prosecuted to the fullest extent of the law. Life in prison. No parole.

Max's company was shut down, and his staff questioned. It turned out most of those he employed were legitimate, and they had no knowledge of the other side of the business.

Not a day had gone by when Raine hadn't thought about her sister. For all the questions that had been answered, many had not. She still didn't know why her sister stepped out on her marriage in the first place, and why she'd lived a double life. Perhaps it was intriguing to her, an escape from what she may have considered a mundane life. But even if she had lived, and the relationship with Max continued, Nora would have spoken up sooner or later. What would her sister's plan have been then?

Since the funerals for Juliette and Seth, Ford had started calling, first to check in to see how Raine and Nora were doing. Then one evening, he asked if he could stop by. He arrived with Chinese takeout and a wooden dollhouse for Nora, which was an instant hit. One evening together became many evenings together, and before long, several months had passed.

As she strolled with Nora to the car, she thought about how much had changed in so little time. They reached the car and

Raine bent down, squeezing Nora's cheek as she said, "What would you like to do now?"

"Can we get ice cream?"

Raine tapped Nora on the nose, nodding. "If it's ice cream you want, it's ice cream you shall have."

"Can Will come too? And can he bring his dog, Sherlock?"

Will.

Raine had called him Ford for so long, she'd almost forgotten it wasn't his first name. She dipped inside the car, glancing at the time on the dashboard.

"I think he's still at work, honey, but why don't we call him and see?"

"Oh-kay."

Raine grabbed her phone and made the call.

When he answered, Raine said, "Your biggest fan requests your presence."

"I believe you mean my *two* biggest fans, right?"

"Right."

"Give me an hour. What would you like to do?"

"Nora wants ice cream, and she's also asking to see Sherlock."

"And what about you? Is there anything *you* need?"

There was one thing.

Ford had asked Raine a month earlier if she'd move in with him, and Raine had needed time to think it over. She'd spent years convinced love wasn't something she could trust again but knowing him had changed that. Tonight, he would get his answer—a confident, resounding *yes.*

THE END

EPILOGUE

Morning light streamed through the tall windows of Montague Manor, spilling across the entryway. Four days had passed since Harlan's arrival, and though Margaret had crossed paths with him several times—over breakfast, in the garden, and once in the sitting room by the fire—he had yet to say a word about the book she'd given him.

Still, she knew he'd been reading.

Each afternoon, as she tidied his room while he was out exploring, she noticed the subtle signs. Once the book had been left open a few pages farther along than the day before, and another time he'd closed it with a bookmark, a few pages farther along still.

At present, Margaret was arranging a vase of late-blooming roses on the front table when the bell on the door chimed.

The door opened to reveal a woman around Harlan's age, dressed in a navy coat and a silk scarf, her auburn hair swept into a loose ponytail.

"Good morning," Margaret said, setting the vase aside. "Can I help you?"

"My name is Opal. My husband, Harlan, is staying here. He invited me to join him. I hope that's all right."

"Yes, of course. He's upstairs. I wasn't expecting—"

"Neither was I," Opal said, as a small laugh escaped her. "He called me last night, and it was the happiest he'd sounded in months."

Before Margaret had a chance to respond, footsteps echoed on the staircase. Harlan appeared, his expression lighting up at the sight of his wife.

"Opal, I'm glad you decided to come," he said.

He crossed the foyer, pulling her in for a warm embrace.

Margaret looked on, feeling a great deal of satisfaction. There was a tenderness in the way he looked at her. Whatever doubts he'd had when he first arrived seemed to have lifted.

"Come on," he said, taking Opal's hand. "I'll show you the room. You'll love it."

As they disappeared up the staircase, Margaret stood for a moment, her thoughts drifting back to the book she'd given him. She wondered if the story had played a role in his decision to invite his wife to join him.

A few minutes later, Harlan returned, offering Margaret a wide grin and saying, "My wife is settling in. I wanted to thank you for the book you loaned me."

Margaret smiled. "Did it speak to you?"

"In more ways than I expected," he said. "I'll admit my emotions got the better of me in some parts, but Juliette's murder and everything that came after made me realize what life would be like without my wife. I thought I could live without her, and now I know I was wrong."

"I'm glad to hear it."

"I finished the book last night, and I called her and told her how I've been feeling. When I finished, she suggested we work together to find our way back to each other. We haven't taken a trip together in years. We've decided to go to Italy. We leave next month. But for now, we'd like to stay a few days longer, if it's all right with you."

"Of course. I look forward to getting to know your wife."

As the sound of Opal's laughter echoed downstairs, Harlan said, "Well, I suppose I'd better go make a plan for today."

He turned, and as he ascended the stairs, a thought crossed Margaret's mind. Perhaps some stories weren't just read, they were lived, rewritten every day by those brave enough to begin again.

THE END

Thank you for reading The Killing Hour, book 2 in the Margaret Montague mystery series. I hope you enjoyed getting to know the characters in this story as much as I enjoyed writing them for you. You can find the series order (as of the date of this printing) in the "Books by Cheryl Bradshaw" section below.

ENJOY THE KILLING HOUR?

You can show your appreciation by leaving a review on Amazon, Barnes & Noble, Apple Books, Google Play, Kobo, or Goodreads.

If you write a review, please be sure to email Cheryl (cheryl@authorcherylbradshaw(dot)com) so she can express her gratitude. She does her best to reply to as many emails as she can, and she appreciates every piece of mail she receives.

ABOUT CHERYL BRADSHAW

Cheryl Bradshaw is a New York Times and 16-time USA Today bestselling author writing in multiple genres, including mystery, thriller, romantic suspense, supernatural suspense, and poetry. She is a Shamus Award finalist for best private eye novel of the year, an eFestival of Words winner for best thriller, and has published over fifty books since 2011.

When she's not writing, Cheryl loves jet-setting to new countries, playing with her grandkids, high tea, and pursuing a wishful side career as a professional food tester of wine and cheese.

NEVER MISS ONE OF
CHERYL'S BOOK'S AGAIN!

Sign up for Cheryl Bradshaw's "Killer Newsletter" today to be the first to know when a new book is released and to enter to win fun bookish swag. You'll also receive some fantastic book freebies just for joining!

Learn more by visiting CherylBradshawStore.Com and adding your email address on the SIGN UP AND SAVE form at the bottom of the home page. Your email in for our eyes only and will not be shared with anyone else.

BOOKS BY CHERYL BRADSHAW

Sloane Monroe Series

Silent as the Grave (Prequel, Book 0)

When the body of Rebecca Barlow is found floating in the lake, private investigator Sloane Monroe takes on her very first homicide.

Black Diamond Death (Book 1)

Charlotte Halliwell has a secret. But before revealing it to her sister, she's found dead.

Murder in Mind (Book 2)

A woman is found murdered, the serial killer's trademark "S" carved into her wrist.

I Have a Secret (Book 3)

Doug Ward has been running from his past for twenty years. But after his fourth whisky of the night, he doesn't want to keep quiet, not anymore.

Stranger in Town (Book 4)

A frantic mother runs down the aisles, searching for her missing daughter. But little Olivia is already gone.

Bed of Bones (Book 5) (USA Today Bestselling Book)

Sometimes even the deepest, darkest secrets find their way to the surface.

Flirting with Danger (Book 5.5) A Sloane Monroe Short Story

A fancy hotel. A weekend getaway. For Sloane Monroe, rest has finally arrived, until the lights go out, a woman screams, and Sloane's nightmare begins.

Hush Now Baby (Book 6) (USA Today Bestselling Book)

Serena Westwood tiptoes to her baby's crib and looks inside, startled to find her newborn son is gone.

Dead of Night (Book 6.5) A Sloane Monroe Short Story

After her mother-in-law is fatally stabbed, Wren is seen fleeing with the bloody knife. Is Wren the killer, or is a dark, scandalous family secret to blame?

Gone Daddy Gone (Book 7) (USA Today Bestselling Book)

A man lurks behind Shelby in the park. Who is he? And why does he have a gun?

Smoke & Mirrors (Book 8) (USA Today Bestselling Book)

Grace Ashby wakes to the sound of a horrifying scream. She races down the hallway, finding her mother's lifeless body on the floor in a pool of blood. Her mother's boyfriend Hugh is hunched over her, but is Hugh really her mother's killer?

...

Sloane Monroe Stories: Deadly Sins

...

Deadly Sins: Sloth (Book 1)

Darryl has been shot, and a mysterious woman is sprawled out on the floor in his hallway. She's dead too. Who is she? And why have they both been murdered?

Deadly Sins: Wrath (Book 2)

Headlights flash through Maddie's car's back windshield, someone following close behind. When her car careens into a nearby tree, the chase comes to an end. But for Maddie, the end is just the beginning.

Deadly Sins: Lust (Book 3)

Marissa Calhoun sits alone on a beach-like swimming hole nestled on Australia's foreshore. Tonight, the lagoon is hers and hers alone. Or is it?

Deadly Sins: Greed (Book 4)

It was just another day for mob boss Giovanni Luciana until he took his car for a drive.

Deadly Sins: Envy (Book 5)

A cryptic message. A missing niece. And only twenty-four hours to pay.

Deadly Sins: Pride (Book 6)

A secret lies within the Kingston mansion's walls, a secret that's about to bring the past into the present.

Deadly Sins: Gluttony (Book 7)

In a town where silence holds its own dark voice, the past has returned, and Gideon Belmont is about to learn an unfortunate lesson.

...

Sloane & Maddie, Peril Awaits (Co-Authored with Janet Fix)

...

The Silent Boy (Book 1)

In the hallway of a local tavern, six-year-old Louie Alvarez waits for his mother to take him home. A scream rips through the air, followed by the sound of a gun being fired. Louie freezes, then turns, with a single thought on his mind: RUN.

The Shadow Children (Book 2)

Within the tunnels of the historic port city of Savannah, fourteen-year-old

Andi Leland has her mind set on freedom—not just for herself but for all the other teens who have come before her.

The Broken Soul (Book 3)

When the party of a lifetime becomes a party to the death, the lines become blurred. Friends become enemies. Drugs become weapons. And that's just the beginning.

The Widow Maker (Book 4)

A friend murdered. A business in trouble. A marriage struggling to survive. And that's just the beginning.

The Familiar Stranger (Book 5)

As semi-retired private detective Sloane Monroe unwinds at a luxurious spa retreat in North Carolina, a jarring phone call shatters her peaceful getaway.

...

Georgiana Germaine Series

...

Little Girl Lost (Book 1)

For the past two years, former detective Georgiana "Gigi" Germaine has been living off the grid, until today, when she hears some disturbing news that shakes her.

Little Lost Secrets (Book 2)

When bones are discovered inside the walls during a home renovation, Georgiana uncovers a secret that's linked to her father's untimely death thirty years earlier.

Little Broken Things (Book 3)

Twenty-year-old Olivia Spencer sits at her desk in her mother's bookshop, dreaming about her upcoming wedding. The store may be closed, but she's not alone, and her dream is about to become her worst nightmare.

Little White Lies (Book 4)

When a serial killer sweeps through the streets of Cambria, California, Georgiana Germaine gets swept up into a tangled web of deception and lies.

Little Tangled Webs (Book 5)

What if you knew the person you loved was murdered, but no one else believed you? Eighteen-year-old Harper Ellis knows she's right, and she's prepared to risk her life to prove it.

Little Shattered Dreams (Book 6)

At fifty-five, Quinn Abernathy has been through her fair share of experiences in life. And tonight, her past is coming back to haunt her.

Little Last Words (Book 7)

After living in a verbally abusive relationship for the past six years, twenty-seven-year-old Penelope Barlow has finally found the courage to leave. But can she escape ... with her life?

Little Buried Secrets (Book 8)

In a split-second, a car collides with Margot, and she finds herself hurdling through the air, her bike going one way as she goes the other. Her mind whirls in this moment, as she thinks about her life and just how much she doesn't want to die.

Little Stolen Memories (Book 9)

In a secluded cabin deep within the woods, an ominous stranger is about to change the lives of six unsuspecting teenagers forever.

Little Empty Promises (Book 10)

As librarian Cordelia Bennett prepares to lock up for the night, a mysterious sound startles her. She turns. The fading light reveals a chilling presence in the shadows, and Cordelia realizes she's not alone.

Little Hidden Fears (Book 11)

Noelle Winters has just thrown the perfect engagement party ... or so she believes. As the evening winds down and the toast is about the commence, the lights go out. And for someone, the night has just turned deadly.

Little Dark Deeds (Book 12)

It's Georgiana Germaine's wedding day. But when one of her closest friends is noticeably absent from the ceremony, Georgiana worries something sinister is to blame.

Little Silent Stranger (Book 13)

Walking the wooded path to her friend's house, Audrey Ashford soon realizes she's not alone. What begins as a familiar shortcut quickly turns into a deadly encounter, and by the time she reaches the ridge, it's far too late.

...

Margaret Montague Series

Eye for Revenge (USA Today Bestselling Book) (Book 1)

Quinn Montgomery wakes to find herself in the hospital. Her childhood best friend Evie is dead, and Evie's four-year-old son witnessed it all. Traumatized over what he saw, he hasn't spoken.

The Killing Hour (USA Today Bestselling Book) (Book 2)

Suburban housewife Juliette Granger has been living a secret life ... a life that's about to turn deadly for everyone she loves.

The Perfect Lie (Book 3)

When true-crime writer Alexandria Weston is found murdered on the last stop of her book tour, fellow writer Joss Jax steps in to investigate.

<u>Hickory Dickory Dead </u>(USA Today Bestselling Book) (Book 4)

Maisie Fezziwig wakes to a harrowing scream outside. Curious, she walks outside to investigate, and Maisie stumbles on a grisly murder that will change her life forever.

...

Addison Lockhart Series

...

Grayson Manor Haunting (Book 1)

When Addison Lockhart inherits Grayson Manor after her mother's untimely death, she unlocks a secret that's been kept hidden for over fifty years.

Rosecliff Manor Haunting (Book 2)

Addison Lockhart jolts awake. The dream had seemed so real. Eleven-year-old twins Vivian and Grace were so full of life, but they couldn't be. They've been dead for over forty years.

Blackthorn Manor Haunting (Book 3)

Addison Lockhart leans over the manor's window, gasping when she feels a hand on her back. She grabs the windowsill to brace herself, but it's too late-- she's already falling.

Belle Manor Haunting (Book 4)

A vehicle barrels through the stop sign, slamming into the car Addison Lockhart is inside before fleeing the scene. Who is the driver of the other car? And what secrets within the walls of Belle Manor will provide the answer?

Crawley Manor Haunting (Book 5)

Something evil is coming. Something dark. Something seeking to destroy everything and everyone in its path. And Addison Lockhart is the only one who can stop it.

...

Till Death do us Part Novella Series

...

Whispers of Murder (Book 1)

It was Isabelle Donnelly's wedding day, a moment in time that should have been the happiest in her life...until it ended in murder.

Echoes of Murder (Book 2)

When two women are found dead at the same wedding, medical examiner Reagan Davenport will stop at nothing to discover the identity of the killer.

...

www.ingramcontent.com/pod-product-compliance
Lightning Source LLC
Chambersburg PA
CBHW071425260626
47170CB00008B/2589